"You didn't tell your *daed* what I said to you, did you?"

"About you not [illegible] y me?" Levi asked. "*N*[illegible] subject. It would just [illegible] tomorrow and see *Da*[illegible] our feelings together."

"We'll see," Verity murmured, the butterflies in her stomach fluttering. "I spoke with my *mudder*. About our marriage."

His laugh surprised her. "I would have loved to have been a fly on the wall for that conversation. She must think Otto's lost his mind, trying to match the two of us in holy matrimony."

"She surprised me. She agrees with Otto. Said she and *Daed* think it's time I remarry. Seems I'm getting stodgy and set in my ways."

"Have you gotten stodgy?"

"You don't want to know what I am, but I'll tell you what I've decided to do."

"Go on."

There's no turning back now. "I will promise to court you, pretend to love you, but that's all for now."

"Your promise is good enough for me."

Cheryl Williford and her veteran husband, Henry, live in South Texas, where they've raised three children and numerous foster children alongside a menagerie of rescued cats, dogs and hamsters. Her love for writing began in a literature class, and now her characters keep her grabbing for paper and pen. She is a member of her local ACFW and CWA chapters, and is a seamstress, watercolorist and loving grandmother.

Books by Cheryl Williford

Love Inspired

Pinecraft Homecomings

Her Secret Amish Child
Their Convenient Amish Marriage

The Amish Widow's Secret
The Amish Midwife's Courtship

Visit the Author Profile page at Harlequin.com.

This book is dedicated to God
and to my two gifted oncologists:
Dr. Dennis L. Rousseau, who performed my
complex cancer surgery in October of 2015, and
Dr. Edsel Lumbca Hesita, who successfully
got me through five months of chemotherapy
in early 2016. Your wisdom saved my life
and kept me writing. God bless you both.

Chapter One

Thunder rumbled in the distance. A peek out the window showed another band of drenching rain coming in from the west.

Finished with a sink of dishes, Verity Schrock wiped the sweat from her face on the sleeve of her dress and hurried out of the steamy kitchen with several ladies following on her heel.

It seemed lately she rushed from one task to another, never finding time to sit down and enjoy a moment of the day.

Fanning her hot face, she quick-stepped down the hall, ready to join the cluster of singers regathering in the great room.

She'd been up since five, long before the old rooster had had a chance to give his first crow of the morning. An experienced cook, she enjoyed the task of making a tower of assorted shoofly pies, a chocolate cake with rich mocha icing, and for herself, a gooey pan of rich golden-brown apple crumble, her favorite dessert.

Taking in a calming breath and clearing her voice, she surveyed the room for the soprano singer's section and found Bunhild, the community's seasonal matchmaker standing in the place she usually occupied. Purposely avoiding the meddling old woman, she slipped into the end of the alto singer's section.

Acting as if she were listening to the song director's instructions, Verity situated herself closer to Clara Hilty, who was making a point of ignoring her best friend since childhood while holding back a fit of giggles behind her petite hand.

With her gaze straight ahead, Verity's finger searched for and found Clara's rib cage, and gave her very pregnant friend a playful poke.

Clara jumped, nearly knocking over the young lady standing in front of her.

Everyone in the lines turned and glared their way.

"Shame on you, Verity," Clara muttered out the side of her mouth.

Verity leaned in close to her friend's ear. "You should have warned me Bunhild showed up for singing practice. I could have hidden in the kitchen closet until she'd left." Putting on a heavy Pennsylvania Dutch accent, Verity held back her own giggles as she muttered in Clara's ear, "Those Lapp *bruders* are still marriage-minded, and looking for a pretty young woman like yourself to wed."

Clara laughed out loud, amused by Verity's rendition of Bunhild's heavy northern accent. Verity couldn't help but laugh with her. For as long as she'd known Clara, which was going on fifteen years, they'd both been consummate pranksters. Nothing had changed now that they were adults.

Still grinning, Clara's arms came up and rested on her rotund stomach. There would soon be a long-awaited first *boppli* for her and her husband, Solomon Hilty. Verity couldn't help but be excited for them—and a little envious. She loved children, especially tiny babies. She had hoped for a half-dozen *kinner* of her own, but *Gott* had other plans for her life and gave her and Mark just the one sweet *dochder*. But she wanted to ignore unhappy memories. Her excitement grew as she thought instead about a new *boppli* in the community to care for and cuddle.

Clara's giggles turned into a delighted smile. "I could have warned you, but it's so much fun watching you squirm under Bunhild's gaze." But then her expression went dead serious. "You know her matchmaking skills are known far and wide, and you being such a young widow makes the opportunity to play matchmaker too tempting for the old girl."

Verity pretended to adjust her *kapp* and readjust the pins holding down her bun, so she would have an excuse to lean in close to Clara again. "You'd better watch out. I could tell Solomon how much you really paid for that new sewing machine you bought off that *Englisch* woman."

Two spaces down, Pinecraft's best solo soprano hissed like a leaky gas valve and gave both women a disapproving glare before going back to listening to Sarah Beth's information on the upcoming fund-raising frolic where they'd be singing at Benky Park.

When Verity looked back, Clara's playful smile was gone. "You wouldn't tell on me?"

"I might," Verity whispered, her eyebrow raised in a mock threat. But she'd never say a word about the extra twenty dollars spent. The seller had kindly thrown in a sewing basket full of threads and four packs of machine needles. A real deal.

Known for his penny-pinching ways, Solomon Hilty would still grumble about the extra money spent. Verity wasn't about to blab, but she ought to. Determined to wed Verity off, Bunhild Yoder was no laughing matter, and now she had to deal with her as soon as singing practice was over.

Feeling eyes on her, Verity glanced up and released an irritated sigh. Bunhild was staring at her again from across the room and wearing that exasperating expression of eternal hope. Verity inwardly cringed. "You know I respect Bunhild's skills as much as everyone in the community, but if I must listen to one more of her sermons on how marriage is *Gott*'s plan for your life, I think I'll scream."

A loud knock at the front door sounded, redirecting Verity's attention. "Whoops! Excuse me." She slipped out of line and hurried to welcome the late singer at the front door. Working as Albert Hilty's live-in housekeeper the last few years had proven to be hard work, but she'd grown to love the aging widower she'd known most of her life and his growing family. Life ran smoothly on the orange grove, which brought a sense of peace to her and her young daughter Faith's lives.

Verity hurried, convinced it was Helen at the door. She often came late to practices, especially if her precious three-month-old *boppli* had once again kept her up with night colic.

"Well, it's about time you got..." Verity's playful words died in her throat at the sight of a tall well-built *Englischer* standing on the porch. He wore tight faded jeans and a white T-shirt that strained to cover his broad chest. A baseball cap perched on his long dishwater-blond hair advertised some brand of soft drink she'd never heard of.

Her heart skipped a beat and then two. Overtly handsome men always made her nervous, like ants crawling all over her skin. This one made her extremely nervous. "Oh, I'm sorry... I thought you were Helen." She took a quick survey of his smiling face and then glanced down at the sleeping dark-haired toddler he held. The pink-cheeked *kind* looked completely out of place next to the man's firm biceps. "Are you looking for Albert or Solomon?"

"Both." He grinned. A dimple appeared in his cheek. "What are you doing here, Verity?"

A chill rushed down her spine. The man's words were spoken in the same husky voice that sometimes disturbed her dreams at night.

"Leviticus?" It didn't seem possible. Now that she took a good look he did seem slightly familiar, but nothing like the young Amish boy she'd loved and promised her heart to all those years ago. How many years had it been since Leviticus abandoned Pinecraft and their engagement plans? *Nine, maybe ten?* Yet here he was on his father's doorstep, activating the nerves in her stomach.

He flashed a full-blown smile at her, again revealing the familiar dimple near his left cheek. "No one's called me Leviticus in a long time. My *Englischer* friends call me Levi."

Her angst against the man revived, even though she thought she'd forgiven him a long time ago. "I'm not one of your *Englisch* friends, Leviticus." She tried hard but couldn't manage to take her eyes off his sun-tanned face and the way his blue eyes twinkled behind familiar thick brown lashes.

She detected an angry red scar running the length of his unshaven right cheek. Her gaze dropped to the blond stubble peppered with ginger covering his chin. When he'd left Pinecraft, there'd been no scar and not much stubble, for that matter. He'd left wearing the plain clothes associated with their strict faith. Today, the man he'd become seemed perfectly comfortable in his *Englischer* clothes and worn-out running shoes.

Averting her eyes, she let him pass through the front door. There were so many reasons why she didn't want him back in Pinecraft. Forefront in her mind was the way he'd broken her heart and abandoned their dream of a life together. *So why is he back?* She motioned him farther into the house. "*Komm.*

Your *daed*'s in the garden. I'll fetch him for you." A slight tremble in her voice revealed more about her irritation toward him than she wanted. She made her way past her mother and several chatting women, ignoring their inquisitive expressions and quiet murmurs as they moved down a long hall that led to the great room.

"Verity, wait." Leviticus tugged at her arm, his fingers barely touching her skin.

Verity looked down at his tanned fingers pressed against the paleness of her arm and sent him a cautionary look. *Don't touch me. Don't you ever touch me again.*

He released his hold, his questioning expression carving lines in his forehead.

She forced herself to relax. It was just Leviticus come home, after all. He meant nothing to her anymore. "You'll find Albert next to the rose garden."

He nodded, and then glanced back at the collection of women clustered in the living room. "Have the women gathered to pray? Is someone sick?"

She shook her head, shoving her trembling hands into her apron pockets to keep her reaction to him hidden. "*Nee*, the church choir is having a singing frolic in the park this weekend. There's been so much destruction in Pinecraft since the hurricane. Some of the women have planned a dinner to raise much-needed funds. Clara was kind enough to offer the choir use of the farmhouse so we could practice."

Verity could still feel the gaze of several choir members on her, watching and wondering. Should she mention to Leviticus that his father had had a stroke less than a month ago and was still in a weakened condition? No. It was best she stayed out of the Hilty family business. She was the housekeeper, after all. Not family. She'd leave that conversation for Albert and his son.

"Who's Clara?" Leviticus's eyebrows knitted together.

She spoke over the sounds of the choir warming up again. "Clara is Solomon's *fraa*. Your brother was courting her when you left, but that was a long time ago. No wonder you've forgotten." *Like you forgot me*, she added silently.

The women began to sing in sweet harmony. The words to "Amazing Grace" filled the old house, reminding her that *Gott* had all things under control. Even this awkward situation with the man who had once been her beloved. She tried to sound casual, like someone who didn't care that the man standing next to her had torn her young heart into a million pieces. "Solomon and Clara are living here now, but it's temporary. Hurricane winds did some interior damage to their *haus* down the grove a few days ago and Albert took them in till it's repaired."

"And you? I guess you're married by now and have your own *haus* and *kinner*." His warm blue-eyed gaze pinned her down like a bug to cardboard.

She went cold inside. She spoke matter-of-factly but was anything but inwardly calm. "*Ya*, I was married to Mark Schrock, but I'm a widow now, with a young *dochder* named

Faith. She's with my younger *schweschders* while I'm busy with the ladies." Her gaze dropped to the child sleeping in his arms.

"I'm sorry about the loss of your husband." His words sounded sincere enough, but in the past, his words had seemed sincere, too. Especially after his mother's funeral, when she was seventeen and he had tried explaining why he was leaving Pinecraft, setting her back on the shelf as if they'd meant nothing to each other. That day he'd rambled on without making a lick of sense, especially when he'd suggested his mother had been overworked by the church and his father until the day she dropped dead from exhaustion. Hadn't he realized women like his mother thrived on being needed and never complained?

The *kind* in his arms stirred and stretched, drawing his attention. Flushed with sleep, the little girl made grunting sounds and then settled down. His blue-eyed gaze roamed the child's face as he tucked a pink blanket in around her chubby legs. A long, slim finger ran lovingly down the side of her rosy cheek.

She caught a glimpse of the baby's pursed pink lips. A trickle of milk seeped from the side of her sweet mouth. At least Leviticus had become responsible enough to keep the child well fed. "I see time's brought changes to all our lives. Is your *fraa* with you?"

He looked her over, his expression calm. "*Nee*. I never married."

He seemed comfortable enough with his statement. Like having a child out of wedlock was an everyday occurrence for *Englisch* men like the one he'd become. "She's a cute *boppli*. What's her name?"

"Naomi, after my *mudder*." He grinned, his beguiling dimple flashing again, tempting her to reach out and touch it as she had a hundred times in the distant past.

He laughed. "I tend to call her Trouble when it's three in the morning and she's screaming blue murder with a wet diaper." He remained warm and friendly, even though Verity knew she had to be frowning his way. His playful personality had always been so irritating, yet so appealing to her.

"Babies are known for waking at the worst times." Drawn in by his smile, she relaxed a tiny bit. She thought of Faith's first year and all the sleep she'd lost rocking her in the chair Mark had fashioned for her before the accident took his life. Sadness replaced her half smile with a frown. "*Komm*, you must be eager to see your *daed* after all these years."

"You don't have to come along with me. It hasn't been that long. I know where the garden is." His tone was gentle, but firm. He stepped past her and out the door without a backward glance.

"It's been longer than you think, Leviticus Hilty," she whispered, dealing with what felt like a dismissal. She watched his long stride eat up the distance between the porch and the wood gate surrounding the rose beds. To his retreating back, she muttered softly, "Much longer."

Clara was suddenly by her side, crowding

her out of the doorway with her big belly. Her friend's brow arched as she asked, "Who's that?"

Leviticus strolled alongside the sheds beside the house, over to where his mother's rose garden bloomed in perfumed profusion. "That's your *bruder*-in-law, Leviticus Hilty."

"How can that be?" Clara's honey-colored eyes widened in surprise. Always nosy, she flicked her *kapp*'s ribbon behind her shoulder and inched closer to the screen door for a better look. "He's not anything like the Leviticus I remember. That man's an *Englischer*."

"*Ya*, he is, but he's Leviticus Hilty all the same." Verity strived to steady herself. Her nerves were jingling like the Christmas bells on Faith's shoes. Leviticus had returned. *So what if he's returned? He no longer means anything to me.*

Verity watched as Leviticus turned toward the backfield of blown-over citrus trees and moved on. His shoulders rounded, no doubt in reaction to the damage stretched out before him.

The grove had been slammed by high winds during the recent late-season hurricane. Squalls of heavy rain had flooded field after field until they were all underwater. The house had been spared, for the most part, but the damage to the grove would be considerable, if not devastating, financially. Verity loved the fields of miniature orange trees, this old house, its family. *How will the grove survive?*

"Solomon's not going to like Leviticus's returning home an *Englischer*. Even now, when an extra hand is needed and appreciated." Clara patted her stomach, as if rubbing it would rid her of the concerns that might upset her *boppli*. "And Albert. Do you think he'll easily forgive his *soh* for leaving the faith and never joining the church?"

"He certain-sure missed him." Verity forced her fisted hands to relax at her sides. "As far as I'm concerned, Leviticus coming home is exactly what Albert *didn't* need.

And bringing a *kind* with him, even though she'll be a blessing, will bring more problems. We've got thirty nosy women in the house, all of whom love to spread rumors. We've got to get rid of them as fast as we can. I can hear them now. Albert's *soh* is home and has brought shame to the community yet again." Verity smiled reassuringly at Clara. "You find a way to get rid of the ladies while I deal with this situation."

Verity opened the screen door and scooted past. Consternation put a frown on her face. *Why had Leviticus chosen now to come home?*

Leviticus hurried along, his thoughts scrambled by the funny games God seemed to allow people to play with their lives. His mother's sudden death, his leaving home, his time at the Amish rescue home, his enlistment into the army. Serving a six-month tour in Afghanistan and nearly dying just days before he was to leave had left him dealing with PTSD.

He would have never guessed Verity, one of the people he'd hurt the most, would be taking care of his aging father. She was no longer a girl, and he had to admit she looked good. Better than good.

She'll never take you back, no matter how forgiving an Amish woman she is. You don't deserve someone like her. Not after what you did.

He was still captivated by the spirited Plain woman with coppery red hair and green eyes that sparkled like jewels, but his leftover feelings would have to be crushed.

She would have been my fraa *if I hadn't left.*

Naomi fussed. His hand trembled as he shaded his daughter's face from the morning sun. A reminder that his PTSD was kicking up. He had to keep using the stress management techniques he learned in the hospital and take his pills regularly. Naomi was so young and vulnerable. Her whole life lay before her. She had only him. Would he be enough? Was he up to raising a daughter by himself?

Deep in thought, he ambled toward the rose garden. Memories of his happy childhood flooded in, tugging at his heartstrings. He visualized his *mamm* clipping off dead rose blooms with care. She'd loved all living things, even him, and he'd seldom earned a day of her devotion.

Perhaps she'd still be alive if he hadn't brought shame to their door with his wild ways. He should have joined the church young and been baptized as she'd asked him. But no. He'd had to live the life that suited him best.

Regret swamped his mind. His father had always held his mother accountable for his inappropriate behavior. Late at night, he'd often heard his parents argue. His older brother, Solomon, never caused tension. Leviticus shrugged in regret and continued to his father's favorite resting place.

It broke him to know his mother would never know he'd grown closer to the Lord, straightened out his ways and returned to Pinecraft, where he belonged. With a *dochder* to bring up, it was far better to return home with tremors from the war than to linger in the *Englischer* world.

He took in a deep breath, the scent of the roses reminding him of who he was meant to become. A Plain man, with Plain ways.

The thick grass underfoot was still marshy from days of torrential rains. He squinted from the bright sun peeking out beneath a cluster of storm clouds. Up ahead his father, Albert, sat in a wooden Adirondack chair, his back to him.

Leviticus walked up quietly, searching for the words he'd practiced repeatedly, but found he'd lost them to the nerves twisting his gut. *"Daed?"* he whispered. *If only speaking Pennsylvania Dutch would make me Amish again.*

A strong gust of wind carried his word and rushed it toward the sea. He stepped closer, fighting the urge to reach out a hand and touch his father's silver hair blowing in the breeze. He had no idea how he'd be received. Like the prodigal son, he'd lived with the pigs and eaten their slop for far too long. It was time he faced his past. But doubt crept in. Would he be forgiven? Could he live the Plain life? *"Daed."*

Albert Hilty's head twisted round, glancing over his shoulder. His smile melted away. A dazed expression crossed his weathered face. He rose with effort, staggering, then reaching out for the arm of his chair. His father's blue eyes blinked, his countenance growing incredulous. "It's you, Leviticus? This time I'm not dreaming?"

"No, *Daed*. You're not dreaming. It's me. Such as I am. I'm home for good if you'll have me." Leviticus waited. A sense of peace came over him, edging out the dread he'd felt at the thought of confessing his sins to his father and the bishop. He was glad to be home, glad he didn't have to deal with the remnants of PTSD alone. He'd needed his family and his growing faith more than he'd realized.

Albert stumbled forward, arms reaching out. He threw himself at his *soh* and clung to him in a warm embrace as he kissed his neck, murmuring, "At last you are home."

As Albert held him, Leviticus could feel his father's frail body trembling. A wave of love washed over him. This old man was more precious to him than he'd realized. For a moment, he couldn't let go. *It's been so long.* He'd been so angry. "I'm sorry I left so abruptly. I thought… Well, it doesn't matter what I thought back then." His head dropped with shame as his father's gaze sought his. "I should have come home sooner."

"*Ya*, you should have." His father nodded in agreement. "Ach, and who is this child between us?" Albert held on to Leviticus's arm for support, considering the face of his grandchild for the first time. The edges of his mouth turned up into a smile.

"This is my *dochder*, Naomi. She's come to see her *grossdaddi*."

Albert appeared bemused for a moment, his thin, graying brows arching down. His gaze locked with Leviticus's. "The *kind* has your *mamm*'s button nose and her name. This is *gut*." He nodded again. "You have a family now. I should have realized you would after all these years." The old man's next words rushed out. "*Welkom* home, Leviticus. You have been sorely missed."

"But not by everyone. I'm sure Otto and some of the elders were glad to see the back of me all those years ago."

Albert squeezed his son's arm. "*Nee*. They prayed for your soul and your safe return home, as I did. But let's forget all that for now. My *soh* is home. *Gott* in His mercy will forgive your past sins if you repent. He who was lost has returned. I care not what others think. Today is a *gut* day. *Komm*, let's go into the *haus*. I want to get better acquainted with my *kinskind*."

Albert shuffled forward, his steps unsure. Leviticus stayed close. *How had* Daed *gotten so weak in a matter of years?* When he'd left, his father had been a strong and able-bodied man.

Leviticus glanced up. Verity hurried to his father's side, supporting him as he took small steps. He leaned heavily on her for strength. How long had his *daed* needed help just to walk? Shame raced through him, burned his cheeks. While he'd been busy living his own life, he'd forgotten time hadn't stood still for his father, or for the grove. Gott *forgive me, I should have never left this place.*

"What happened to you, *Daed*?"

Verity supported his father by the arm. Her eyes surveyed Leviticus, saying, *It's too late to be concerned now. You should have stayed home.*

Her arm around his waist, Verity assisted Albert up the back steps and through the kitchen door. The old man shuffled over to the table and sat with a loud sigh, then wiped sweat off his face with the swipe of a bandanna he carried in his back pocket.

Verity stood by the sink, her hand pressed to her throat, a worried frown creasing her forehead. His gaze shifted between her and his father.

Albert smiled. He spoke, as much to himself as anyone. "That *Englischer* doctor said I had a stroke a while back." He shook his head. "*Nee.* I don't see how he could suggest such a thing. I can still walk and talk just fine."

Leviticus pulled out a chair at the kitchen table next to his father and lowered himself, watching the aged man's every move, seeing confusion cross his father's wrinkled face.

Albert's age-spotted hand smoothed the tablecloth in front of him. "I'm certain-sure most folks can't walk or talk after a stroke." He smiled Leviticus's way, one side of the old man's mouth slightly drooping. "Verity can tell you. I'm doing mighty fine for an old man of seventy plus years. Ain't so?"

Verity locked eyes with Leviticus and shook her head, encouraging him not to correct his father's misconceptions. She reheated the coffee she'd made for herself a few minutes before and laced a cup with two scoops of sugar to ward off Albert's shock. "He's doing fine now that he's up and about." She placed her hand on Albert's shoulder and set a cup of sweet coffee in front of him.

"Would you like something hot to drink?"

"Sure." Coffee sounded good. Leviticus took off his billed cap and placed it on the table, revealing his windblown, long blond hair that grew down around his collar.

Verity's mouth pursed, her disapproval narrowing her green eyes. Once he changed his clothes to Amish and had his hair cut around his ears he'd fit in better.

There'd been a time when he'd fit in fine, belonged...regardless of how rebellious he'd become. He was one of them. But now? The loss of who he could have been caused his heart to ache. *What must* Daed *be thinking?*

Verity poured another cup of coffee and set the steaming mug in front of him. As she went back to the stove, Leviticus could hear his new sister-in-law ushering the last of the singers out the front door. The pregnant woman's nervous giggles told him she was doing her best to avoid saying too much about his appearance and the suddenly shortened choir practice.

A glance at the battery-run clock over the stove told him it was high noon. Solomon would probably be home soon for his lunch. Leviticus feared his return wouldn't bode well with his hardworking *bruder*. There'd be enough gossip flying around the community about his homecoming without the ladies spreading tales of a heated argument between him and Solomon.

Verity swatted wisps of hair away from her forehead and then lowered her head, concentrating on making hearty roast beef sandwiches for the men. Albert slurped his coffee as he always did. Leviticus remained quiet for a moment, observing and remembering. Verity stole a glance his way as the *kind* in his arms began to fret. Naomi's pudgy bare feet kicked the air in agitation.

"She needs a diaper change. Any chance my old room's still available?"

"It is." Verity cut into a ripe tomato and took out all the seeds for Albert's sandwich.

Everything was different. Never in a million years had he imagined he would someday come home and have need of a cot for a *boppli*. Nothing had prepared him for the shock of seeing his father so emaciated. Not even the war.

"I've got a small porta-cot Faith used stored under my bed. I'll wipe it down and put it up in a minute, just in case she gets sleepy again."

Albert's head bobbed. "*Ya*. Use your old room, *soh*, but leave the *kind* and such things to Verity. She's had plenty of experience with *kinner* of all ages. Ain't so?"

Verity raised her chin and nodded.

He was sure she had taken care of many children, but this one was his and another woman's child. There'd been a time that fact would have hurt her beyond measure. From the glare she was giving him now, Leviticus could see he was no longer important to her.

"*Ya*, I'll see to the *boppli*, if that's all right with her *daed*."

Leviticus lifted his shoulders in a half shrug. "I had thought…"

Albert tugged at his beard, watching him as he shifted Naomi to his shoulder and soothed her.

"A woman knows what's best for *bopplis*. I'm surprised Naomi's *mamm*'s not here, seeing to her needs. Will she come later?"

Leviticus straightened out his daughter's pink collar. "*Nee*. Julie's not coming. She's a judge advocate of some importance. Her job keeps her busy in Washington. We're not married, *Daed*. When Naomi was born, Julie made it clear she wanted nothing further to do with me or our *dochder*."

His *daed*'s eyebrows shot up. The room became silent, as if time stood still. Albert sat soundlessly digesting Leviticus's disturbing words. "This woman, Julie. She is *Englisch*, *ya*?" He scratched at his beard, his deep-set eyes surveying Leviticus closely.

"She is."

"That explains the lack of a wedding." Albert took a sip of coffee. "*Nee* Plain woman would walk away from her *kind* and leave a *mann* to care for it. *Gut* thing you came home. Naomi will be well loved here on the grove." Albert twisted in his chair, his bony hand motioning Verity over. "*Komm*, lunch can wait. The *boppli* needs a woman's touch."

Leviticus's gaze locked with Verity's as she lifted the *kind* from his arms. She nodded, their silent conversation missed by Albert. She would take good care of his child. Naomi whimpered and pushed away as she was taken out of her father's arms. Without a backward glance, Verity made her way through the kitchen door, into the great room.

Albert followed his housekeeper with his eyes. "She's had a hard few years, Leviticus. I think a husband is what she needs. Someone to carry the load of parenting with her. You've been away a long time. People change. Just go easy if you have a mind to court her again."

Leviticus dropped his head. What his father said was true. He and Verity had been over for a long time. And in the condition he was in, she was off-limits to him. He'd make sure of that. She deserved someone whole. Not a man who fought night terrors and jumped every time he heard a loud noise.

He couldn't help but think about the way Verity used to look at him, like he was something special. Today that look had been replaced with indifference, but who could blame her? She had forgiven him for breaking her heart, but not forgotten. He was sure of that. True, it was her nature to forgive. But she wore her heart on her sleeve and always had.

Yet, it was evident by her disapproving expression that she had no feelings left for him. He was just someone to be tolerated now. He was Albert's son, but not her lost love.

Chapter Two

Leviticus finished the sandwiches Verity had started and served one to his father before settling down with his own. His thoughts stayed on Naomi as he chewed. She was in good hands, but had Verity noticed Naomi was a squirmer? Less than a year old, she needed to be closely watched or she'd be rolling off the bed and onto the floor.

"*Danki, soh.*" Albert pulled the well-filled sandwich closer. "There's chips in the larder, if you have a taste for them."

"*Nee.* This is fine."

"My doctor said no more greasy foods

for me, but Verity lets me have baked chips occasionally."

"She treats you well, then?" Leviticus's gaze focused on his father's pale skin, noticing the way his heart beat fast in a vein on his neck.

"*Ya*, Verity treats me special *gut*." Albert took a small bite of his sandwich and began to chew.

In truth, time hadn't stood still for either of them. His father's eyes were on him, too, judging what he saw and probably finding fault with his clothes, the scar running down his cheek that screamed violence. But if his father *was* disappointed, he said nothing as he ate several bites and then pushed his half-eaten sandwich away. "My appetite isn't what it used to be."

"*Nee*. Mine, either." Leviticus glanced around the sunny kitchen. Some things remained as he remembered them. The same pot rack held his *mamm*'s old cookware. The pot holders she'd made from spare quilting blocks hung from the same golden hooks. A familiar set of plastic canisters sat against the back wall on the counter. His *mamm*'s indecipherable handwriting labeled them as flour, sugar and coffee. Memories of her love and care caused him pain and added regret. She had been a woman of tiny stature, barely the size of a twelve-year-old child. But what she lacked in height, she made up for in spirit and determination.

He could still picture her scurrying around this room, preparing meals fit for a king. Her spunk kept him out of trouble with the elders during *rumspringa.* She'd always expected the best from everyone and gave back in kind. But he'd stolen, lied and drank too much during his time of running around, bringing her nothing but disgrace in the end. Shame ate at him, burned his throat. Had the stress been the reason she'd died so suddenly, and not hard work?

Leviticus stored away his memories. His father didn't need to see him cry on his first day home. "You want a glass of water?"

"*Ya*, sure. *Danki.* I need to take my pill."

Albert opened one of the brown medicine bottles on the table and laughed. "I never thought I'd find myself pushing pills in my mouth morning and night, but Verity says she'll tell the doctor if I don't take them on time."

He turned toward his *soh*, his expression incredulous. "You know, the doctor put me in an *Englischer* nursing home for three whole days after my stroke. But Otto sent Verity along. She pulled me out and brought me home, just like a *gut dochder* would do. I had to laugh at all her bluster and spirit, her bright copper hair flying wild about her *kapp* like she was *Gott*'s emissary come to rescue me."

Albert guffawed. "Certain-sure she saved me from the grip of the enemy." His head bobbed. "*Ya*, for certain-sure." He set the bottle of pills he'd been holding on the table. "She's been my right hand since that day, and a fine housekeeper, too." He laughed again. "That girl has spunk. Just like your *mamm*. You should have married her while you had the chance."

Leviticus knew he should have. He should have done a lot of things better than he had. Some had paid too high a price for his having his own way. He desperately needed *Gott* to show him mercy, remove the horrific dreams of war, the remains of PTSD still plaguing his mind from time to time. Would redemption remove his every sin as his bishop had preached when he was young? For now, he would live with the guilt burning his insides until God removed the pain. His father's forgiveness would go a long way toward securing a measure of peace for his troubled mind.

Footsteps crossing the small wooden porch out back told him Solomon would soon be walking in through the back door. No doubt hungry and expecting Clara to be fixing his meal.

Leviticus prepared himself for their confrontation. Solomon had every right to be livid with him. A young man of twenty, he'd been left to deal with the grove, with a father set in his ways and growing feeble with age and illness. Had there been too little money to hire fruit pickers to help run the land, buy what was needed the last ten years?

The back door handle turned and Solomon stepped in. His brother had grown taller, put on a little weight and seemed fit under his traditional Amish garb. Brown hair, so much like their *mamm*'s, ran riot over his head. Windblown clusters of curls poked out from under the dirty straw work hat that he wore. Dried mud caked his boots up to his dark trouser cuffs.

Solomon stopped in his tracks, taking a long, hard look at Leviticus. His blue eyes narrowed as he realized who stood by his father's side.

"What's he doing here? Did you send for him?"

Albert accepted the glass of tap water from his younger son's hand and swallowed his pill. *"Danki."* His eyes cut to his oldest son. "Now, how could I have sent for Leviticus? I didn't know where he was any more than you did. *Gott* directed your *bruder*'s steps home."

Leviticus watched the exchange. Albert seemed calm and steady, but Solomon's face reddened, ready to explode with fury.

Leviticus stepped forward.

Solomon turned toward him, ignored Leviticus's outstretched hand. His finger jabbed toward the back door. "Get out! You're not *welkom* here."

Albert swayed to his feet. His face flushed a ruby red. "I'm still alive and owner of this grove, Solomon Hilty. Leviticus is my youngest *bu*. He can stay as long as he chooses, and you have *nee* say in if he comes or goes."

Solomon banged his fist down hard on the wooden kitchen table, rattling their coffee mugs. "Where was your precious *soh* when the orange trees dropped fruit from fungus? Remember how we worked twelve-hour days to save that crop?"

Solomon's loudly spoken words echoed

through the house, a verbal slap across Leviticus's face. He'd earned that slap…and more.

"Where was Leviticus when you almost died in the grove?" He pointed to his *bruder*. "Did he come and sit by your hospital bed for days? *Nee*. But I was there, *Daed*." Solomon's finger poked his own chest. His tone dropped, tears glistening in his eyes. "I was there the whole time."

"You were there and that was as it should be. But your *bruder* is home now. You should be happy Leviticus has come to make things right with *Gott*. Hasn't that always been our prayer?"

Looks were exchanged between brothers. Leviticus's frayed nerves shouted at him to run, leave all the drama behind and just go. Solomon didn't understand why he'd left, but now was not the time for explaining. He'd done enough damage to this family.

Solomon has a right to want me gone. If the roles were reversed, I'd be saying the same to him.

Two steps brought Solomon to his father's side. "Is that what he told you? That he's come home to give *Gott* and the Amish way of life a chance? Do his long hair, his *Englisch* clothes look like a *mann* ready to turn over a new leaf, *Daed*? Do they?"

"This will end now!" Verity stood in the doorway, her eyes wide and spitting fire. "Your *daed* has no need of this foolishness. I will not have him made upset."

Solomon flashed a look at Leviticus that spoke volumes. He slammed his work hat back on his head. "This is not over, little *bruder*. Not by a long shot. The bishop and I will talk and then you'll be gone." He slammed out the door, the glass pane trembling in his wake.

Barefoot, Clara entered the room from the hall and flashed past Leviticus, her advanced pregnancy evident by the round bulge pushing at the waistline of her plain blue dress. Tears ran down her face as she rushed out the back door behind Solomon.

Leviticus took a sip of his water, swallowed hard and poured the rest of it down the sink. He'd expected Solomon to be relentless with anger and he hadn't been far off the mark. Solomon's forgiveness might come, but not today. Maybe not ever.

Her face flushed, Verity patted Albert on the arm. "You'll be all right while I gather the eggs?"

"*Ya*, sure. Leviticus is here now. He can fetch and carry for me till you're back in."

She nodded but paused a step away and turned back. "You took your pill?"

"*Ya*. Just like you told me. One at lunch and the other at dinner."

"Gut." Verity grabbed the egg basket and then hurried out of the room, but not before sending Leviticus a warning glance over her shoulder that told him she wouldn't put up with any more foolishness from him around his father.

Leviticus raked his fingers through his tangled hair and let his arm drop to his side. Verity wasn't comfortable with him around, either. What had he expected? A happy homecoming? Like Solomon, she may never forgive him.

Albert motioned for him to sit. "Your *bruder*'s angry now, but he'll calm down. It may take time, but he'll see the error of his ways and repent. I taught you both how to forgive, as *Gott* forgives us." He smiled at his youngest *soh*, his eyes lighting up.

"Your *bruder* missed you. He's just bone tired and frustrated. The hurricane—it did terrible damage to the grove." Albert rubbed at the base of his neck. "We're not sure the grove can be saved. A big city buyer came round today, offering fifty cents on the dollar for the ground, but Solomon ran him off before I could." The old man thrust his fist in the air. "I'll die before I see this grove given away." He laid his hand on his son's arm. "Now that you are home, there is hope for the future of Hilty Groves."

"Don't put your faith in me, *Daed*. Trust in *Gott*. I'll disappoint you every time." Humiliation ripped at his gut. He hadn't earned his father's trust yet, but he would, given time. He didn't know if he had what it took to be the kind of *soh* his *daed* needed him to be, but he intended to try. *Can I become a Plain man and please* Gott?

Somewhere in the dark room, a baby was crying as if its heart were broken.

Verity woke disoriented, her jumbled thoughts convincing her it was Faith's lusty waïls. She hurried out of bed, hoping she could calm the *boppli* before her cries woke Mark. He rose early each morning, before the sun's first rays. *The poor* mann *needs his rest.*

She frantically searched for her robe at the foot of the bed, then went on a hunt for her missing slipper. Kneeling, she found it just under the bed. Verity rushed to scoop the baby up, but the cot wasn't where it should be by the back window. She turned, looking about in the darkness. The whole room seemed off-kilter, everything out of place. Why wasn't the night-light glowing? She always left it on, so she could check the baby without disturbing Mark. Had the bulb burned out?

She located a lamp on the dresser and switched it on. Its golden glow flooded the room.

She glanced around. One side of the bed was rumpled. The other empty.

Reality returned like the jab of a knife. She let out a loud sigh, all the while her heart pounding in her throat. Mark was with the Lord, his broken body deep under the soggy ground, along with their tiny *soh*, who'd been born much too early due to her shock and grief.

The crying child was sweet Naomi, Leviticus's child.

Her house shoes made scuffing noises as she hurried across the hardwood floor and lifted the squirming child into her arms. Naomi was furious, her face red and splotched from crying. Her feet kicked the air in outrage. Verity cooed and softly talked to her, trying her best to calm the irate *kind*.

She and Leviticus could have had their

own *dochder* if he hadn't walked away. But he had. Faith's birth had filled her with a mother's love, but what about Naomi? The child needed the care and love of a *mamm*. But could she care for Naomi and not feel resentment? A look into the baby's shimmering dark eyes told Verity all she needed to know. She would love Leviticus's child and show no grudge.

She hugged the child closer, even though Naomi protested and pushed away. All *kinner* needed to feel wanted. Especially this bundle, whose *mamm* thought more of her job than her own flesh and blood. Anger rose up. Her heart ached for Naomi. How could anyone disown such a sweet *boppli*?

Soaked from head to toe, Naomi was inconsolable. Her diaper, sheet and blanket would need changing. She'd have to put a fresh diaper and gown on the *kind* before she could get the chill off a bottle of milk.

She worked fast, stripping off the *Englischer* onesie covered in tiny orange giraffes and pink rabbits. Amish children slept in nightgowns made of soft cotton, as was the custom. She'd made all her daughter's gowns by hand and packed them up as Faith outgrew them. They'd been stored away for her next *kind*, but that *boppli*, a son she'd named Aaron, had lived but a few hours and then taken his last breath. Out of the dozens of gowns she'd sewed for him, he'd only worn one while alive. He'd been buried in a casket gown made by her hands, his little body swallowed up in the tiny garment painstakingly sewn while she'd cried a million tears in sorrow.

Aaron had never gazed into his mother's eyes or fed at her breast. The loss of Mark had left her broken, but the loss of Aaron had left her inconsolable. Almost crazy with grief, she'd shaken her fist at God the day they laid Aaron in the ground. She still asked how her *soh*'s loss could have been *Gott*'s will. Nothing good ever came from his death.

A tap sounded at her closed bedroom door. Bending over the foot of her bed,

Verity quickly wrapped Naomi in a blanket and picked her up before cracking the door. *"Ya?"*

Leviticus stood just outside the semidarkness of her room. As if he'd dressed in a hurry, his shirt was buttoned incorrectly and thrown over wrinkled jeans. His long hair stood out wild around his sleep-creased face.

"I heard the baby crying and thought you might need my help."

"You could fix her bottle while I redress her." Her nerves tensed. *Leviticus shouldn't be in my bedroom while the others sleep on.* She edged back to her bed, drawing Naomi close to her as she went. The child squirmed, almost slipping out of her hands. Turning her back to Leviticus, she tried to still the child's body as she wiped her down with wipes and grabbed for a fresh diaper.

Leviticus stood over her. "She squirms a lot."

Uncomfortable with the closeness of their

bodies, she dipped her head, her eyes on his *kind. "Ya."*

He stepped away. "You'll have to be extra cautious when changing her near the edge of the bed. She's quick."

"That she is." Glad he'd moved toward the door, she couldn't help but grin. His *dochder*'s wiggling antics reminded her so much of Faith at this age.

"I'll be right back." And with that, Leviticus was gone, his shape melting into the darkness of the long hall.

After a moment, she could hear him in the kitchen, clanging pans and opening cupboards. Verity pondered his predicament. Leviticus seemed practiced in things pertaining to his *dochder*'s care. She had never met a man who could tend to a little one's needs. Not that Mark hadn't shown an interest in everything she had done for Faith. But to have expected him to go for a warm bottle or change her? She chuckled aloud at the thought. Amish men didn't do such things unless their *fraa* was ill and there was no one else to help, which was seldom the case in Pinecraft.

Before she could slip on and snap together Naomi's one-piece sleeper, Leviticus was by her side, shaking the warm baby bottle with gusto. "The nurse I hired said to shake the formula really well."

"*Ya*, but I don't think she meant you to make whipped cream of the milk." She held out her hand and took the bottle, avoiding his fingers, even though a secret part of her longed to touch him. She tested the warmth of the milk on her wrist before settling herself and the child in the small rocker in the corner.

Leviticus stood looking at them, his expression undecipherable in the shadowy room.

"You can go back to bed now. I can manage."

He reached back, blindly searching for the doorknob, and stepped out with a nod. Silence filled the room. The muted sounds of Naomi smacking down her milk brought calm to Verity's soul. She began to hum one of the songs she would sing to Faith. Movement caused Verity to look back toward the door. Leviticus had returned, partially hidden in the gloom. "Go. I'll take good care of her. There's no need for you to worry."

Would he ever go away?

"I know you will, but it's hard for me to let go."

"You don't have to let go completely. Just trust me to see to her needs. To love her like she deserves to be loved."

"Why would you want to do this for me after the pain I've caused you?"

Verity rested her head back against the rocker, her eyes closed. The weight of the baby was a comfort to her empty arms. The soothing motion of the rocker brought needed peace. "My caring for Naomi has nothing to do with what went on between us. Naomi needs me. I'll see to her needs. Any woman would."

"Not every woman. Her own *mamm* wouldn't." He stepped out of the shadows, into the light. "How can a *mudder* feel nothing for her own flesh and blood?" Leviticus's expression was bleak.

Anger gripped her. She fought down the compassion she felt growing for him. She couldn't fathom any woman being so heartless. "I have no answers for you. You'll have to ask Naomi's *mudder* the next time you see her."

The lamp's muted glow turned his hair to spun gold. "Do you mind me asking what happened to your husband?" He leaned against the doorjamb, waiting for her reply.

She took in a quiet breath, prepared to tell the story once again. Each time she had to speak of her husband's death, her loss grew. "Mark was a hard worker, a *gut* man. New to Pinecraft, he took a job with a local arborist. He was still in training when he climbed up a tree and fell to his death." She sighed. "No one was at fault. He somehow managed to put on his harness incorrectly. It didn't hold when a rotten branch broke and fell on top of him."

"I'm sorry for your loss."

Verity nodded. She couldn't speak for a moment. Leviticus's words seemed sincere enough, but his regret didn't mean a thing to her. All those years ago, he'd sounded sincere when he'd told her he loved her, too. But he hadn't. Not really. He'd left her standing next to his *mamm*'s grave, with everyone looking on as he tenderly kissed her lips and walked away without so much as a backward glance.

Tears gathered in her eyes. "Morning comes early around here, Leviticus. Get to bed." Verity spoke carefully, keeping her tears from falling. When he finally shut the door behind him, she let her tears flow. She cried for Naomi's loss, for her loss of Mark and for her *soh*, who'd never known his *mamm*'s love. But she refused to cry for Leviticus. He'd earned his pain, even though something, that small voice, told her she was wrong.

Chapter Three

Golden rays of sunlight rose above the groves. The gray sky overhead had turned into a cloudless blue day.

Shredded palm fronds and broken tree branches littered the big fenced-in yard. Leviticus turned back toward the house. Roof tiles and tar paper added to the debris near the rambling dwelling he'd grown up in. There was a lot of work to be done and not many community hands available to help, thanks to the widespread damage around town.

He stepped inside the kitchen door, nodded at Verity, who was busy working at the end of the counter, and then smiled at his father, who was eating at the breakfast table.

"*Gut mariye*, Leviticus. Did you sleep well?"

"*Mariye, Daed.*" He knew he was breaking one of his *mamm*'s cardinal rules when he slathered his hands with dish soap and rinsed them in the sink meant only for washing dishes, subconsciously hoping she'd appear and scold him one more time for misbehaving. "I slept well enough, I guess." He dismissed the night terrors he'd endured that had woken him with muffled screams. Verity and his father didn't need to know about the remnants of PTSD that still haunted him night and day.

Verity gave him a disapproving glance for abusing the sink but went about her business, cutting fresh fruit into chunks. She didn't say a word of greeting. There were dark circles under her eyes. *Had Naomi kept her up crying?* The first weeks he'd cared for Naomi, he'd had his own share of sleepless nights. Google called the problem a mix-up of days and nights. He'd called exhaustion a miserable way to live.

Perhaps Naomi missed her mother. He thought of Julie, wondered how she was feeling now that the *boppli* was gone from her life forever. She'd had six months to bond with her own flesh and blood, even though the nanny seemed in charge of Naomi the day he'd been around. He'd never seen Julie pick up Naomi once or feed her, and she'd said no goodbyes to her when they'd left.

Leviticus grabbed a cereal bowl out of the cupboard and took a spoon from the freshly washed dishes on the drain board and then pulled out a chair and sat close to his hard-of-hearing father. He grimaced as he poured cereal from the plastic container and noticed moon-shaped, colored rainbows coated in sugar.

Verity stepped beside him carrying a cutting board of fruit. "You sure you don't want oatmeal?"

He shook his head. "*Nee*. This will do fine."

She put some of the fruit on his father's

hot cereal. Leviticus's head lifted in surprise when Albert dug into the tan gooey mush with all the gusto of a small boy. Some things *had* seriously changed around the grove. When his mother was alive, his father had his oatmeal with brown sugar and lots of butter, but that was how she'd made it for her husband and his father never complained or asked for anything different.

Leviticus ate a crunchy bite of the sickeningly sweet cereal and held back a groan of disgust. A sugar rush was just what he didn't need, but he wasn't going to be a bother to Verity. She had enough to do; besides, she was rushing around like she was in a hurry. "Where's everyone?" He ate another bite of cereal, determined to make it through at least half the bowl.

Verity flipped over a perfectly fried egg. "Solomon left for the grove over an hour ago, and Clara's still sleeping. Solomon said she had a rough night of it. The *boppli* kept her up with all its movements."

His thoughts went back to Julie. He'd

left for his six-month tour in Afghanistan right after she'd learned she was pregnant. While he was gone, he'd missed out on her strange cravings, the sight of her belly growing round with his child. He'd been cheated out of Naomi's first few months of life, too. He could thank his injuries and lengthy hospital stay for that.

Forget Julie. Naomi was home among family now. That was all that mattered.

Albert tipped his coffee mug and drained the last drops of his dark brew. "I thought we'd take the ATV out and inspect the grove's damage for ourselves. Solomon says it's extensive, but until I see it for myself I can't come up with a plan for how to fix it."

Verity cleared her throat and finished drying her hands as she spoke. "Solomon called Otto before he left. Seems the packing plant was flattened by the high winds. No one's sure if they'll be rebuilding it anytime soon."

Albert shoved back his chair and rose. "I'm certain-sure Thomas will do the right thing. He'll put the building up again with the help of the community." He edged toward the sink and put his bowl among the other dishes needing to be washed. "Amish and *Englisch* alike depend on him."

His shoulders dropped, his head shaking. "I don't know what we'll do if he chooses to close the business for *gut*." Staring into space, he tugged at his beard, using the kitchen counter as support.

Verity dusted down her apron and adjusted the cleaning scarf on her head. "Otto's going to see how many men he can gather but warned he might not find enough to make much of a difference. There's a lot of damage done to the houses in the district. Everyone's busy caring for their own *familye* needs first. Some Plain folk have hired *Englisch* laborers."

Her concern for Albert showed in the dark circles under her eyes, the way her shoulders sloped from the heavy weight of responsibility on her shoulders. Had she considered what would happen to her job if the grove closed? Who would be her mainstay if it did?

Albert grinned. "Don't underestimate that ole bishop's ability to gather a crowd. He can still be a persuasive man when the need arises." Albert used the sturdy kitchen table as a crutch as he maneuvered back to his chair. "You send Otto along to me when he gets here, Leviticus. We'll head out to the grove as soon as he comes."

Leviticus quickly finished the last spoonful of cereal he could stomach and rose, his eyes on Verity. "You'll have time to see to Naomi's needs?"

She dished up a bowl of oatmeal for herself and sat on the far side of the table across from his *daed*. "*Ya*, she'll be sleeping for a while yet. She took her bottle without a fuss at six and went straight back to sleep."

"I noticed you found the duffel bag of baby clothes I left by your bedroom door yesterday."

She poured milk over her oatmeal, added a heaping teaspoon of brown sugar and then tossed a handful of blueberries over the top.

"I did. *Danki.*" She returned his gaze. "I hope the rain holds off. She'll need the cloth diapers I have dried. I've used up most all the disposable ones you had in the diaper bag, and the spare store-bought ones I had left over from Faith."

"Speaking of Faith, when's the *kind* coming home?" Albert poured himself a half-cup of coffee and splashed in milk.

"*Mamm* said she'd bring her back this morning, but I figure I'll see them later in the day." Verity smiled Albert's way. "Today's cherry vanilla day at Olaf's Creamery. It's Faith's favorite flavor. *Mamm*'s sure to get her a scoop before leaving town." Verity's smile brightened. "*Mamm*'s got a half-dozen grandkids and another on the way, but you'd think Faith was her only *kinskind* the way she spoils her."

Leviticus watched Verity's eyes light up as she spoke about her daughter, saw the worried lines vanish from her face. She was the old Verity in that moment. The girl he'd once loved and never deserved.

"Does your little girl like *bopplis*?" Would Verity have enough energy to see to two active *kinner* after the difficult night with Naomi?

Verity sent a rare, genuine smile his way. "Faith loves *kinner* of any age. In fact, she's always asking when I'm going to get her a baby *schweschder*."

Albert guffawed into his tall mug as he slurped down the last of his coffee. "You've got to lower your standards and marry again for that to happen." His teasing expression was a welcomed sight, but he became serious once more. "No *kind* should grow up alone."

Rising, her hands on her hips, Verity looked poised to react negatively to Albert's words, but the sounds of several ATVs and an *Englischer* van pulling to a stop on the graveled driveway outside stymied her words.

Leviticus glanced out the window. Otto and Mose Fischer piled out of a black van and headed toward the house. Several men, some he didn't recognize, followed close behind. Solomon got off his ATV and walked over to the bishop. He jerked his head toward the house, his face pinched, no doubt still fuming. Was his *bruder* informing Otto of his homecoming? The aging bishop looked toward the back door and nodded, his steps lively as he approached. Mose trailed not far behind. There would be questions asked. Hard ones. He prayed he'd have the right answers for the man of God.

Albert slid out of his chair, his hand reaching for the door. He slipped outside just as the thump of their boots sounded on the porch. Pulling his gaze away from the window, Leviticus put his water glass in the sink and braced himself. As a young man, he'd gotten along with Mose Fischer, the bishop's son, just fine. But Otto, the local New Order bishop? Not so much. They'd had their run-ins, and Leviticus knew he would have been shunned if he'd been a member of the church during his restless time.

But he was different now, willing to accept the Amish way of life. With *Gott*'s help, he'd figure out what the Plain life meant for him.

The slam of the front door and sounds of muffled laughter sent Verity skittering past Leviticus, down the long hall that led to the great room, her bare feet slapping against the wooden slats of the floor as she hurried along. Faith was home, and she needed to tell the little girl about Leviticus's arrival and the *boppli* he had brought with him.

Her gaze sought out Faith. Dribbles of strawberry ice cream marked the skirt of her *dochder*'s pale pink dress. Verity smiled her welcome to her *mamm*, but her eyes were drawn back to her Faith. "I see someone got ice cream."

In her childish version of Pennsylvania Dutch, Faith exclaimed, "The ice cream was so *gut*. *Grossmammi* let me have two scoops." Verity kneeled, and Faith hugged her *mamm* round the neck, almost pulling Verity down with her excitement.

Verity accepted a shower of kisses from Faith while removing her slipping cape and outer *kapp*. "You must have been a special *gut* girl to get such a treat."

Faith's head bobbed up and down with enthusiasm, her messy bun at the base of her head bouncing, ready to fall without the support of her everyday *kapp* to keep it secured. "*Grossmammi* said I was so *gut* that we could go see the new puppies at Chicken John's after Thanksgiving. They're too little to touch just yet." Faith's big brown eyes grew wide with excitement and anticipation. "Can we go see them soon?" Verity's heart melted with love for her *dochder*, but she shot her *mamm* a frustrated glance. When would she have time to care for a small dog underfoot?

Verity's *mamm* laughed at Verity's serious expression and silent warning. "It's just to look, Verity. It's not like I promised Faith she could have one."

"Maybe your *grossmammi* and I should talk about your visit to Chicken Joe's while you go change your dress." Verity tucked Faith's lightweight winter cape and *kapp* under her arm, searched for and found her *dochder*'s white everyday *kapp* hanging from her small fingers. She quickly tidied Faith's bun but didn't attempt to replace the head covering. "There. Now, scoot. Change your dress. And mind you don't run..." Verity's last words became a whisper of frustration as Faith took off in a flash of pink down the hall, headed, no doubt, to the kitchen to find Albert.

Verity turned to her mother. "A puppy, *Mamm*? Seriously? That's the last thing I need right now. I'll have to be the one who tells her she can't have it. Not you."

"She doesn't ask for much, Verity."

Verity dropped her head, wishing she could relax her hold on life and enjoy it like she had when Mark was alive. "Leviticus has returned home, much to our surprise. I'd best go catch Faith before she starts giving him the third degree. You know how she is with strangers." Her trembling hands sought refuge in her apron pocket as she hurried off. Her mother was right. Faith didn't ask for much. Just love and a small fuzzy puppy.

Chapter Four

Waiting for his father to return to the house, Leviticus glanced toward the arch of the kitchen door as a petite, barefoot little girl ran into the room, her hair a cluster of wild ginger curls escaping from her bun, much like her *mamm*'s hair often did. Her big brown eyes sparkled in the sunlight streaming in through the kitchen window. The *kind* stopped abruptly and gave him a look of surprise and awe.

"Are you my new *daed*?" The child's gaze penetrated every fiber of his being, into his very soul. A sprinkling of honey-colored freckles disappeared when she scrunched up her nose and grinned impishly, exposing two missing bottom teeth. "I told *Gott* I wanted a blond-haired *daed.* He got that part right, but you've got blue eyes. I wanted a *daed* with brown eyes, like me." Her crinkled brow and piercing gaze suggested disappointment, but her smile returned quick enough.

Leviticus couldn't help but laugh out loud as the mixed emotions flashed across her face. He knew an imp when he saw one, and Faith Schrock was that and more. "I apologize. I do have blue eyes, but that's okay, because I'm sure *Gott*'s still debating on who's to be your new *daed.*"

"*Nee*, he sent me you. He just got the eye color wrong." Bareheaded, the child wore a traditional pink Amish dress and apron, but her miniature *kapp* hung from her delicate fingertips.

"Shouldn't you be wearing that *kapp* on your head?"

"*Nee*, my *grossmammi* said it could stay off. She got tired of pinning it back on this morning." Her grin grew into a full-blown smile. "Do you think I'm hopeless?"

"No, I think you're adorable."

Her grin widened. "Did you bring my *bop-pli* with you?" Faith moved forward one step and then another, her hands busy situating a cloth doll under the crook of her arm.

"I'm assuming you asked *Gott* for a *bop-pli*, too?"

"Not a baby. A *boppli schweschder*. One like Beatrice has. She won't let me hold hers." Her bottom lip poked out in a pout. "She said I might break her, but I wouldn't."

Verity and a woman he recognized as her *mamm*, Miriam, came into the room. Verity reached for Faith's hand and pulled her to her side. Her troubled gaze pierced him. "I'm sorry. I should have warned you. My *dochder* is a real *blabbermaul*. She doesn't understand it's not okay to speak to strang-ers."

Faith buried her face in her mother's skirt for a moment and then laughed as she sprang forward, exposing her toothless grin again.

"He's not a stranger, *Mamm*. *Gott* sent him to me. He's my new *daed*."

Verity flushed red. She knelt and spoke quietly, the smile she had for her *dochder* staying firmly in place. "A week ago you said *Gott* sent the garbage man to be your new *daed*. I'm confused. Which is it going to be?"

"Him," Faith declared with all the conviction a small child could muster and pointed Leviticus's way.

Emotions tore through him. What kind of father would he make if he was this *kind*'s *daed*? One day Naomi would be just like Verity's little girl. Full of life and silly questions. He'd have to step up. Find a way to be all Naomi needed him to be.

Longing tugged at his heart, and for a moment, he allowed himself to imagine parenting two delightful little girls with Verity. When they were teens, Verity had said she wanted a house full of children. Back then, he'd had everything a young man could want. They could have become a happy *familye*. But rebellion and grief had pushed him away and left him the shell of the man he was. Verity had been better off with the man she'd married, this Mark she spoke of in such high regard.

He took in a deep breath, watching the girl. He couldn't encourage her childish dreams. *Gott* would have to rebuild him if he was to be all he could be. Gott *grant me wisdom. Show me the way.*

Verity smiled at her daughter, her thoughts on Leviticus. Some might have missed the momentary flash of alarm that crossed Leviticus's face, but Verity hadn't. She had no intention of pursuing him as she had when she was young.

Kinner had a knack for coming up with the most ridiculous ideas. If he didn't understand that yet, he would soon, now that he had a *dochder* of his own to raise. Verity squeezed her eyes shut for several seconds, gathering her thoughts, tempering her annoyance.

She concentrated on Faith, who was smiling bright and impatiently waiting for her *mamm*'s response. "*Nee*, I'm sorry, my *lieb*. Leviticus can't be your *daed*. Not today, or any other day. He already has a *familye*. He has a precious *dochder* named Naomi to raise."

Faith's face crumpled, prepared to cry. "But why can't I be his *dochder*, too?" She pulled away from her mother and jerked round to face Leviticus, her small hands placed on her slim hips. "Right? Your *bop-pli* can be my *schweschder*. We can be a *familye* just as I prayed?"

Leviticus approached the child slowly, his gaze touching on Verity and then back to Faith. His words were spoken soft and easy to the child as he kneeled in front of her. No doubt his words were said for Faith's benefit and hers. "I'm just starting to learn what it is to be a *daed*, Faith. I'm not very good at dealing with little ones yet. It would probably be best if you prayed some more. Ask *Gott* for someone with a bit more experience with *kinner*. You shouldn't have any problem finding your *mamm* a husband since she's so pretty."

The back door opened, the squeaky hinges heralding Otto Fischer's entrance.

"Leviticus?"

Verity took Faith's hand and hurried out of the kitchen. Leviticus had opened the floodgates of retribution on his own head. Let him deal with it alone.

Disturbed by Faith's comments, Leviticus tried to gather his thoughts as he stood with a nod directed toward the old man making his way around his father. A senior citizen now, the old bishop still moved with purpose and authority, like some of the generals Leviticus had served under. Otto always had a way of carrying himself with dignity, but without any of the pomp and ceremony used by the four-star generals. If he lived to be a hundred, Leviticus would never know the kind of veneration Otto and the officers had earned.

He recalled being a *bu* of ten and being

called into Otto's study for stealing candy from Old Dog Troyer's five-and-dime store. He felt the same ripple of trepidation curl his stomach now as the Amish bishop's piercing blue-eyed gaze turned on him, hard and steely. A bad case of nerves had his hands shaking. More than anything, he didn't want to be sent away, back to the *Englisch* world.

Otto muttered something to Albert and Mose on the porch, and then quietly shut the door, leaving them alone in the kitchen.

Otto spoke, his accent still heavy with the same Pennsylvania Dutch inflection his father and many of the old ones used. "It is *gut* to see you, *soh*. I'd feared you were lost to us when you walked away." Otto pulled out a kitchen chair with a gnarled arthritic hand and motioned Leviticus over with a wave.

Habit almost had him saluting and clicking his heels together at attention. His respect for the man was that strong now that he'd matured into an adult. He lowered himself into a chair. "*Gott* taught me hard lessons and brought me home with my tail between my legs."

"Perhaps you were in the pigsty, bruised and battered for a time, but not harmed beyond repair. Ain't so? It is *gut* you came back when you did. Your *daed* grows frail and needs you more than ever. This grove needs you, too. Solomon is one man. He can only do so much." Otto tugged at his beard, gave Leviticus's *Englisch* clothes a thorough once-over. The man's hairy brows rose with disapproval. "Is it your intention to join the church and be baptized right away, or will you continue to fight the will of *Gott* and make your *familye* grieve further?"

The restrictions of military life had brought about much needed changes in Leviticus, but still, making the choice to be a Plain man wasn't coming easy to him. He was making the choice mainly for Naomi, he told himself, but deep inside he knew better.

He understood the need for rules and uniformity better now, but he still didn't like the feeling of being boxed in and held to guidelines he didn't always agree with. No doubt, he would find it hard to live by the community's strict *Ordnung*, but he could endure anything for his *dochder*. She'd need a stable *familye*, people to love her, and this tiny community could provide all that. "Yes. I realize the Amish way of life is best for me."

Otto's hand stilled on his beard. His eyes narrowed. "I'm told you have a *dochder*, but I see no *fraa* at your side."

"That's right." His mouth went dry, but he managed to hold Otto's piercing gaze. He had repented to God for his relationship with Julie but refused to be ashamed of Naomi's existence.

"And is there a plan in motion? Someone you have in mind to marry, see to your *dochder*'s needs? Children can be a heavy burden for a *mann* with no *fraa*, no matter how much they love their *kinner*." Otto settled back in his chair, not giving Leviticus a chance to answer his questions before he started speaking again. "It makes me wonder if an arranged marriage would be the best solution. There will be several eligible women coming to the community during the winter season. Perhaps you've considered this yourself and have already thought of someone suitable?"

Leviticus worked his jaw, not sure what to say. He had assumed Verity would continue to see to Naomi while he worked with his father and brother in the grove. "Verity—"

"*Ya*, this is a *gut* plan. Verity will make a fine *fraa* for you. She is a broad-minded woman with spirit. And her *dochder* needs a *daed*." Otto nodded, a half smile curving his lips. "Verity was a *gut fraa* to Mark Schrock, and she will be faithful to you, too. Albert is already used to her ways, and content to have her around. You've made a *gut* choice." Otto nodded vigorously. "Wasn't there a time of walking about for you and Verity? An engagement, even? Perhaps bans were read in church?"

Alarms went off in Leviticus's head. Sure,

he needed a babysitter or full-time nanny, but a *fraa*? He wasn't prepared to court *any-one* just yet. Not the way he was, and especially not Verity. It was apparent she still held a grudge against him for leaving her all those years ago. And who could blame her? He rose and shoved his trembling hands in his jeans pockets. "We did court for a time, but—"

"There's no need to be troubled about the lack of remaining emotional attachment, if that's what's concerning you. Love will return, given time. Once you're schooled, become a member of the church and are baptized, we can set the wedding date for December or sooner. With an immediate engagement, Verity's family will have no need to be concerned about her reputation."

"Her reputation? But Verity and I haven't picked up where we left off." His heart raced, almost thumping out of his chest. Things were moving too fast. He needed time to think, time to consider what would work for all involved. Certainly not this foolishness. What would Verity say?

Otto watched his every move and gesture, reading into it what he would. It was the man's nature to scrutinize people. He spoke firmly, his look fierce. "You can't expect Verity to live in this *haus* with you, a single *mann*, and not be touched by local gossip. She must stay. Albert can't do without her. Not with his health still so unpredictable. *Nee*, one of Verity's unmarried *bruders* must come and live on the grove until the wedding." Otto nodded, deep in thought. "*Ya*, this is all *gut*."

The sound of an ATV motor's revving brought Otto to his feet. He moved toward the back door. "*Komm.* We must go. We'll discuss this later in the day, after we've surveyed the damage to the grove." He clasped his hand on Leviticus's shoulder and squeezed. "I'm sure, given time, Verity will agree to a quick marriage of convenience and all will be settled."

Leviticus followed close behind Otto, his feet

dragging and thoughts frantic. What *would* Verity think about this situation they found themselves in? Trapped in an Amish till-death-do-us-part trap. *Thanks to my big mouth.*

Chapter Five

Verity did her best to slip a clean cloth diaper under Naomi's bottom, but the *kind* squirmed and fought valiantly, insisting she be allowed to roll on her belly and crawl away. "You'd best be still, little *schatzi*, before we both get stuck by this pin."

She smiled and then laughed out loud as the *boppli* babbled and attempted conversation. Naomi's easy-to-read eyes expressed sheer joy at the trouble she was causing and resisted the distracting kisses Verity tried to rain down on the *kind*'s forehead and nose.

Clara came into the bedroom and inched in beside the cot. She helped hold the roly-poly *boppli* down long enough for Verity to close the big diaper pins and pull a tiny dress over the *kind*'s head. With a laugh in her voice, Clara asked, "Where's Faith?"

"Sulking in her room."

Her hip supported by the edge of Verity's double bed, Clara slipped off her shoes and sat, her swollen ankles crossed. "What did she do?"

"The usual. Got *lippy* with me and didn't want to take *nee* for an answer."

Verity lifted Naomi out of her bed, kissed the child's soft curls and then moved to the rocking chair.

Clara covered her toes with the hem of her long skirt and settled in for one of their girlie talks. "I expected to find you out of sorts and ready to explode."

Verity raised her chin, her forehead wrinkled. "Why would you think that? I've changed a million diapers in my life. What's one more?" Verity offered a warm bottle to Naomi and grinned as the *kind* reached out and jerked the food toward her rosebud mouth. Her pudgy fingers grasped the bottle and held on tight.

"So you're all for it?"

"For what?" Verity looked closely at her frowning friend. "Is this one of your jokes?"

Clara's expression turned perplexed. "You can take my word for it. I wouldn't kid about something as serious as this. Why in the world hasn't someone told you? I thought for sure the bishop, or at least Leviticus, would ask you if you were all right with the proposition."

Verity leaned forward, careful not to jostle Naomi, her interest piqued. "What proposition? I don't have a clue what you're talking about. It sounds like I need to be told about this scheme since it involves me."

Clara slipped off the bed and with some effort shoved her feet back into her plain black shoes. "Maybe it would be best if someone else explained it to you. I really didn't overhear everything, even though Otto does tend to talk loudly."

Clara tried to slip out of the room, but Verity latched onto the hem of her friend's dress and tugged her back in. She loved Solomon's wife and Leviticus's sister-in-law as much as she loved her own sisters, but sometimes Clara's teasing and nosy ways drove her to distraction. "Sit! Tell me what you know."

Clara's eyes twinkled innocently. "Seriously. I didn't hear much of what was said. And besides, I could have gotten it wrong." She laughed, but the sound held a nervous edge. "You know how rattle-brained I am." She jerked her skirt away from Verity's grasp and inched toward the door.

"Please tell me."

Clara's pace slowed. She shrugged. "But… I'm not sure I should be the one to tell you."

Their gazes met and held. Verity's brows knitted.

Clara reluctantly shuffled back to the bed and sat on the edge with a bounce of defeat. She refused to meet Verity's hard stare. She thrust her hands into her apron pockets and they stayed there.

Verity rose and stood over her. "Once this

boppli finishes her bottle I'm going to go find Otto and ask what all the excitement's about. He might be interested in hearing you're spreading gossip again." She wouldn't tell on Clara, knew her friend loved a good tongue wag, but one way or another she was going to find out what was up.

"*Nee*, don't do that! He'll know what I was doing. Solomon's warned me to stop listening in on other people's conversations. Otto's sure to preach on the sin of eavesdropping come Sunday service."

"Then tell me."

"Has anyone ever told you that you can be a very hard woman, Verity Schrock?" Clara's pink lips pouted, but her eyes glowed with excitement as she began talking. "I was just standing by the door, minding my own business, innocently waiting for Albert to move away so I could go in the house." Slightly top-heavy with child, Clara slid a hand out of her pocket and placed it against her gyrating stomach.

"*Ya*, I think we've established you were

snooping at the door, seeing what you could see and hearing what you could hear. So, go on."

Clara grunted her displeasure at Verity's less-than-gracious remark. "Otto found out about Naomi not having a *mamm*. Since Leviticus has no *fraa* to care for the *boppli*, Otto asked how he planned on managing the daily grind of the grove with a *kind* on his hip."

Nerves tingled up Verity's spine. She didn't like where this conversation was going. "And?"

Clara's eyes became liquid virtue. "Leviticus didn't seem to have a permanent solution and hem-hawed around a bit." The volume of her normally loud voice lowered to a whisper. "You know how fond Otto is of arranged marriages, especially since his and Theda's worked out so well."

"*Ya*, theirs was one of the blessed ones. But what has this got to do with me?" Verity took in a long, cleansing breath. Clara could test the patience of the Lord Himself.

"Is this one of your jokes or another chance to spread gossip?"

Clara's shoulders stiffened. Her eyes narrowed with indignation.

I've hit a nerve.

"*Nee*, of course it's no joke. This really does concern you and if you'll be quiet long enough I'll tell you the rest."

"Seriously, Clara. Talk." Verity pulled the empty bottle from Naomi's damp lips and placed the child's chubby body against her shoulder. She patted and rubbed the *kind*'s back, hoping to lull her back to sleep. "Tell me *only* the parts of conversation that concern me."

Clara nodded, her grin mischievous. "Otto suggested an arranged marriage for Leviticus." She leaned forward. "You should have been there to see his face when Otto explained his plan. I thought Leviticus was going to swallow his own tongue."

A strange sensation gripped Verity's stomach. She sighed. Her impatience grew by the minute. "Please, repeat only the parts that involve me, Clara."

"If you'd stop interrupting I might be able to get to the good bits." Clara's brow arched. "Leviticus blurted out your name when pressured about a prospective *mamm* for Naomi, and Otto became as happy as a child on Christmas morn." Clara smiled. "I mean he smiled a really big, robust smile and nodded a lot, convinced Leviticus's plan was to marry you. By then, Leviticus looked ready to throw up, his eyes bulging like a fresh-caught catfish." A grin flashed at the corners of Clara's mouth, but she went back to nattering, then got serious again. "Otto asked if you two had courted back in the day."

"That was a long time ago." Verity's stomach clenched tighter, not liking what she was hearing. "I no longer have a romantic interest in Albert's *soh*."

"*Ya*, well, you might want to dig up some of those old feelings, because Otto already has your wedding date planned for the month of December."

A trembling began in Verity's legs and crept up to her arms. It took every ounce of willpower she had to keep herself standing. "Are you sure of this? You couldn't have gotten my name mixed up with someone else's?"

"*Nee*, it was you, all right. Otto even mentioned what a sensible woman you've always been."

Verity's mouth became so dry she could barely get her words out. *Sensible. Ha! I'll show him sensible.* "And Leviticus agreed to this marriage arrangement?"

"Well, he didn't belabor the point, or say *nee*. They both walked past me a moment later, and I did notice Leviticus looked red in the face and flustered."

Verity fought for breath. Everyone in their small community knew about Otto's fondness for arranged marriages, but she'd never dreamed she'd become one of his victims.

Hysteria rose and built to a crescendo pitch until she thought she'd scream out loud.

"Don't you utter a word of this to anyone else, you hear me, Clara Hilty?"

Clara chuckled, making Verity's tension grow. She gave up trying to make sense of what her friend had just said. Drawing in a deep breath, she looked down at Naomi. The child was sleeping peacefully in her arms. She felt compassion for the tiny girl, but not enough to get herself tangled up with a half *Englisch*, half Amish man. *We Amish marry forever. There would be no divorce.*

"I may be a sensible woman, but I won't be railroaded into a loveless marriage. Otto will just have to understand and make other arrangements."

"You *are* single and *do* need a *daed* for Faith. Otto may give you an argument."

Verity gave a dismissive wave of her hand. "He can argue all he wants. Unless *Gott* Himself sends a message from heaven, I won't be marrying Leviticus Hilty come December."

Verity jumped when the back door slammed

shut and Mose Fischer began urgently calling her name. Leaving Naomi with Clara, she hurried through the hall but stopped short when she entered the kitchen and saw the washed-out look on the big man's face. "What's happened?"

"It's Albert. He's been rushed to the hospital."

Sitting behind the wheel, Leviticus waited for Mose to come out of the house and jump in the back after alerting Verity. The back door slammed, and Leviticus watched as Mose, followed by Verity, flew over to the passenger side where Albert sat slumped on the truck's bench seat, his head resting against Solomon's shoulder.

The truck rocked as Mose jumped into the back. Solomon took the time to roll the window down, so he could address Verity's fears. "I'm sorry but we have to go. There's no time for explanations. I'll call you as soon as I know something."

"But wait. What's happened? Is it another stroke?" Verity's voice was high with anxiety.

"We don't know. Leviticus and I were speaking and *Daed* just slumped over. Now, *nee* more talk. We've got to go."

Leviticus glanced in his rearview mirror as they sped away, gravel flying from under the fast-spinning wheels of the truck. Verity stood alone in the distance, her skirt blowing in the wind. She needed someone to comfort her. He inwardly groaned. She'd have words to say when she found out he and Solomon had been arguing.

Leviticus pulled his attention back to driving and turned onto the main road. Tempted to speed, he made his way through the traffic, his eyes glancing over to Solomon from time to time. His *bruder* held up their dad's body as best he could. What fools they'd been for arguing over differing opinions in front of their frail father. Stress was the last thing Albert needed.

Regret tore at Leviticus. He couldn't seem to do anything right. Perhaps he'd come home too late to make peace with his brother. As *kinner* they'd been close, shared a strong bond. But now? Now they were strangers and he had no one to blame but himself. He'd been a fool to leave his family, his community. Especially his faith. *Gott* had taught him many lessons, all of them hard to stomach now that he saw the foolishness of his actions all those years ago. If he'd had issues with the way his *mamm* was treated, he should have spoken up, tried to change his father's mind-set. To Albert, hard work was expected of all Amish. Both men and women. It was their way. But his mother's failing health might have been avoided with rest and time to do what pleased her. He pictured his mother, her face smiling in whatever task she took on. Had he been too young to see how content she was?

His time with the *Englisch* had taught him many things, some good, but most not. He'd talk to his father if given the chance. Clear the air between them. God willing, he'd have the opportunity. Another glance at his father's pallor warned him not to take too much for granted. There was no promise his *daed* would live through this latest heath scare. No promise at all.

Father, I release Daed*'s fate into Your hands. Forgive my doubt. Heal my mind. Give me strength to deal with whatever lies ahead.*

Chapter Six

The noxious scent of chemicals and disinfectant hung heavy in the air.

Leviticus could smell it, and wondered if Solomon could, too. He put his hands over his ears, trying to block out the sound of the nurse's squeaking shoes, the conversations all around him. Someone's heart monitor beeped loud and fast. It could have been hooked up to him, his heart was beating so hard. Hospitals brought back memories he'd buried deep and didn't want uncovered.

Slumped in a chair across the hallway, Solomon cleared his throat. Leviticus looked up. Blue eyes that had once sparkled with mischief as a *bu* now appeared gray and lifeless, his mouth an angry slash. Sand and mud stains covered his brother's trousers up to his bent knees. Leviticus looked down at his own casual pants, at his borrowed boots caked in mud. They'd brought the muck and mire of the flooded grove into the hospital with them after their father had fallen ill.

Solomon hadn't spoken a word since they'd arrived with their *daed* in tow. Not even as they waited in ICU while Albert was being worked on. Hours passed and still the silence continued. Leviticus didn't have to be told that Solomon blamed him for their father's sudden attack.

Almost an hour later, Albert was moved from ICU and put into a room on the third floor. He and Solomon had been asked to wait outside the room while their *daed* was hooked up to a fresh IV and monitor. They'd been told there were more tests to be run before they could be sure whether it had been another ministroke.

Footsteps sounded down the hall. Solomon's head lifted.

Leviticus glanced up, expecting it to be Otto rejoining them. He'd gone downstairs for coffee. But when he looked, he saw Verity threading her way past a large family crowding the hallway. She appeared stressed, her usual tidy appearance forgotten. *Just what she needs. Something else to stress over.*

"I left the *kinner* with Clara and got a ride with Mose. Is there any news?"

She was pale and shaking. Leviticus could see Verity's nerves were stretched to the breaking point.

Always thoughtful, Solomon patted the chair next to him and slid his arm around Verity's shoulders when she sat.

Leviticus balled his fists, not liking the familiarity of his brother's touch. Verity was a widow; she was to be treated with respect. Strong feelings of protection washed over him, not that he had any claim on her. She was her own person, someone who'd forgotten him and married another man. Had he expected her to wait until he got his head screwed on tight?

He calmed himself. His brother was being compassionate, not flirtatious. Post-Traumatic Stress Disorder brought on strange and bewildering moods and added internal drama he had a hard time understanding.

Solomon spoke in hushed tones. "*Nee*, there's no news yet. But I've seen this before with *Daed*. He's had another stroke."

A tear trailing down Verity's cheek. She lifted her shoulders in a half shrug. "*Ya*, I thought as much. Mose Fischer said Albert was unable to use his right side. Was the damage to the grove so devastating that the sight shocked him?"

Leviticus waited for Solomon's reply. He knew their bickering back and forth was responsible for their father's sudden stroke.

"The crop's in a bad way." Solomon massaged the back of his neck with long fingers caked in mud. "But that's not what set *Daed* off. It was Leviticus and I arguing. We didn't agree on replanting trees." His forehead furrowed with emotion.

Rekindled regret? Leviticus was dealing with plenty of regrets of his own.

Leviticus spoke up. "*Daed* said the trees should come out and be replanted. I found fault in his wisdom and said so. I suggested we plow up the land and plant hay as some are doing around the state."

Verity rubbed her temples. "Is it possible your *daed* is right? Can the grove be saved?"

Leviticus didn't care if Solomon wanted to hear his opinion again or not. "*Ya*, *Daed* was probably right. The grove could be replanted. It'll just take more work. Most of the serious damage is in the small grove on the east. Fresh dirt can be brought in to strengthen the roots and keep fungus away. We can plant peach and plumb trees where the soil's been eroded."

Solomon bristled. "Is this your *Englischer* wisdom, Leviticus? *Daed*'s plan is sound, but do you have any suggestions on how we'll pay for all this replanting and soil replacement?"

"I didn't tell *Daed* yet, but I have money saved."

"We don't need your *Englischer* money." Solomon's glare was challenging.

Overwrought, both men slipped out of their chairs and circled each other like birds of prey.

Verity rose and touched Leviticus on the shoulder. "If this is how you two acted today, no wonder your *daed* had another stroke." She pointed to the chairs behind them. "Both of you sit down and gather your wits."

Like a wayward child, Leviticus sat, and Solomon soon followed his lead. Verity was right. He and Solomon swiping at each other only compounded their problems. What fools they'd been. "I'm sorry, Solomon. Forgive me."

"Ask *Gott* to forgive you, *Englischer.* I have no pity for you. I only have pity for my *daed.* The grove is ours. Not yours. You never loved the land like *Daed* and I. We'll figure this out without you once you're gone and he's well enough. Go back to where you came from. There is no inheritance here for you, no one to cling to."

"*Was ist letz?*" Otto's brows snapped together as he approached, his frustration showing in his tone and stance. He stood near them, feet planted wide apart. "Is it not enough that you put your *vadder* in the hospital? Do you want to kill him, too? No more squabbles." He threw up his arms in frustration. "Who is right and who is wrong? Such foolishness out of two grown men! Stay seated and be silent."

Leviticus buried his hands in his hair, struggling to pull himself together. Everything Solomon had said was true. How could he expect him to understand his restlessness back then? He couldn't understand it himself.

But he had changed since the war. Death all around had a way of making what was important crystal clear. His faith, his *fami-*

lye and the grove were important now. His newly found desire to put his faith in the Lord had pulled him home, and he was bound and determined to stay in God's will this time around. The grove would continue. "You're right, Otto. This is no time—"

"Albert is all that matters now," Otto interrupted. "Both of you must work together to keep his dream alive. He needs a reason to live." The old bishop shrugged, his broad shoulders drooping. "Once he's gone, you two can fight over the land and settle your difference any way you like. But for now, there will be peace." His tone was serious, his look penetrating.

Solomon held Otto's gaze, hostility draining from his face. "*Ya*, we both hear. No more fighting. This is a time for prayer and renewed hope. Forgive me."

Leviticus tugged at his collar, smoothed down the front of his dirt-smeared shirt. He watched tears well up in Verity's eyes, but then she turned away, displeasure for him written in the wrinkles on her forehead. He could always find a way to disappoint her without even trying. "I'm sorry for acting such a fool, Verity."

Otto gave both men a frosty appraisal. "Has the doctor returned with results?"

Verity turned back, her eyes glistening with tears. "*Nee*, there's no news."

"Then we sit and wait." Otto slid into a narrow chair and made himself comfortable.

Leviticus didn't need test results to know what was wrong with his father. He'd seen it before in Afghanistan. Stress did terrible things to a body. His father was under a burden too heavy for any man his age to carry. He'd had a stroke all right, but just how bad a stroke had yet to be proven.

The clock on the wall ticked off each passing second, though each seemed an hour long. Leviticus finally asked, "The children? How are they?"

"They're *gut*. Clara promised to take them to my *mudder* and *schweschders* to be seen to."

"*Danki.*" Leviticus bent his head low, listened to the heartbeat of the hospital. Were these his father's last hours? Only *Gott* knew for sure, and He was being very silent.

Have mercy on my father, Lord.

Verity slipped into Albert's dimly lit hospital room alone. She'd left Solomon and Leviticus to deal with the bishop's anger.

She paused just inside the hospital room, letting her eyes adjust before shutting the door behind her. One by one, she took halting steps toward the single bed in the middle of the room. The nurse had instructed her not to wake Albert if he was asleep. Was she prepared to see him paralyzed? Unable to walk and talk?

She took three more hesitant steps. Pale, his breath shallow, Albert lay on his back, deep in sleep under a white sheet and a lightweight blanket of pale blue cotton. The oxygen tube positioned under his nose hissed. He snored lightly, the familiar sounds giving her a measure of comfort. The monitor on the wall showed his heartbeat was strong, but sometimes erratic. He looked almost serene—but what did she know about recovering from strokes, heart attacks and such matters? Nothing. An hour ago, she'd read a pamphlet about heart disease and strokes, but its words did little to reassure her. Instead, they scared the life out of her.

She glanced around Albert's bed. He was connected to lines plugged into the machines that buzzed and clicked around him. *There must be a way to keep his blood pressure under control at home, so this won't happen again.* Her hand trembled as she touched his arm, the side of his face. He felt warm, not cold and clammy as she'd expected.

Years ago, her *mamm* had had problems with high blood pressure while pregnant with Mary, the fourth of her *mamm*'s *dochders*. But her problems had been nothing as serious as this.

During that time Verity had become familiar with beeping heart monitors and at-the-ready call buttons that worked much like *Englischer* phones.

She sighed, longing to talk to Albert, needing to know he was all right.

Light from the hall momentarily flooded the room. She glanced around and saw Leviticus slip in. She stepped deeper into the shadows. His gaze sought out his father. He moved forward, slow and steady. She couldn't tell what his expression was, but she heard him sniff, as if he was holding back tears.

Not wanting to intrude, she stayed at the foot of the bed and quietly lowered herself into the hardback chair against the wall. Had Leviticus seen her when he'd come in? She didn't think so. *Let him have his moment with his* daed. *He deserves that much.*

"I'm sorry, *Daed*." His voice cracked and was barely audible. "Please don't die. I need you in my life…in Naomi's."

Verity's heart skipped a beat. As Leviticus moved to touch Albert, she rose, placing a hand on his arm. "Don't wake him. The nurse said he needs his sleep."

Leviticus whirled round, a hand reaching for his heart. “I didn’t know you were in here.”

“*Nee*, I didn’t think so.” She gave a half smile. She’d scared him like he used to scare her a hundred times a day as *kinner*. Their relationship had always been fraught with teasing words and battle cries. Today was no different.

“My words were private. Meant for my father.”

Shame on you, her conscience murmured. She lost her smug, self-satisfied smile, ashamed. *He’s dealing with his father almost dying, and here you are starting up a cat-and-mouse game from the past*. “I’m sorry. That was insensitive of me.”

A scant smile turned up his lip. “It was, but it was so like the old Verity I knew.” His expression turned serious again. “How does he look to you?”

She moved over to the head of the bed, leaving a gap between them. “He’s a shade pale, but otherwise looks *gut* to me, like he's going to wake up at any moment and ask what all the fuss is about."

"I thought he looked *gut*, too. I wondered if it was just my wishful thinking." He chuckled ruefully, his hand rubbing at the rough stubble on his chin. "When do you think the doctor will be back?"

"Probably not until morning, unless the tests they just did reveal something sinister." She put her hand on Albert's bed. She needed to feel a connection to the sick old man.

"Do the nurses know we're still waiting for answers?"

She smoothed out the sheet under her fingers. "*Ya*, they know. Last time it took two days to finish all the tests and get back most of the results."

He took a step closer to be heard by Verity. "What exactly are they looking for?"

His breath brushed past her, tickling her neck. "They're trying to figure out why he keeps having strokes."

Leviticus moved away from her. "It's me

coming home so suddenly, isn't it? I should go, find someplace else to raise Naomi."

"Nee!" Albert's word was soft and slightly slurred, but he managed to get his point across.

Leviticus bent, his fingers reaching for his father's limp hand.

"Di u sell er?" Albert pushed out the slurred words, his face contorted.

"No, *Daed*! Don't talk. The nurse wants you to remain quiet. You need rest. Go back to sleep." Tears rolled down Leviticus's face and dropped onto the front of his mud-spattered shirt.

"Ell er!" Albert lifted his left arm and let it drop.

"Tell me what?" Verity's heartbeat kicked up and began to race. *What could be so important that Albert demand she be told?*

Leviticus stiffened. "He's confused, doesn't know what he's saying."

Albert's hand lifted inches off the bed, his finger pointing Verity's way.

Verity tugged at Leviticus's arm. "Tell

me what you're holding back. You're up-setting him."

"Are you sure, *Daed*?"

Albert blinked rapidly.

"Just remember I tried to stop this foolishness." Leviticus tugged at his shirt collar, undid a button at the neck of his throat. He didn't look directly at her as he spoke. "Otto has a plan and *Daed* agrees with him."

A funny sensation hit the pit of her stomach. Clara had heard correctly. She knew what Leviticus was about to say. "What plan?"

He cleared his throat, and then spoke loud enough for his father to hear, too. "Otto has decided it's best we marry for the children's sake."

"I can't believe you'd even consider..." She couldn't breathe, couldn't swallow. Dry mouthed, she forced her tongue to form the words screaming in her head. "There's no way I'm marrying you."

"Ya." Albert stumbled over the word,

but it was clear this marriage was what he wanted for them.

Verity considered Leviticus's expression and saw the same trapped emotions she was feeling. She became aware of her body trembling, rocking back and forth. Uncontrolled tears coursed down her face, into her ears. "This is your will for my life, Albert?" She held her breath. He nodded. Her heart sank.

Hysteria bubbled just under the surface. There was no way she would marry Leviticus Hilty. Not even for their *kinner*. She had her little girl's future to think of, and the man standing in front of her would have been her last choice. Leviticus hadn't changed. He'd never been dependable.

There had to be a way out. She went to speak, but nothing came out. She wasn't going to upset Albert. For now there was nothing to do but shut up and play along. At least until she found a way out of this insanity. Certainly, Albert wouldn't expect her to go through with the wedding once he was better and thinking clearly.

Breathless, she whispered, “If that is what you want, I’ll marry your *soh.*” Deep inside, she knew. Oh, yes. She knew. This marriage to Leviticus would never happen.

Chapter Seven

Albert's hospital door opened. Leviticus rose from the chair he'd retreated to. His gaze followed a tiny, dark-haired woman as she flipped on the overhead light and walked in the room with Otto by her side. A cream-colored chart tucked under her arm and a black stethoscope dangling from her oversize lab coat pocket told him who she was.

Solomon, who had slipped in moments before, appeared to be surprised, no doubt by the attending physician's gender. Leviticus's army experience had taught him women in the *Englischer* world could rise to high position and rank. He'd risk a guess the young, attractive woman standing a few feet away was the head cardiologist they'd all been waiting for.

Otto shuffled to the foot of the bed, his black hat in hand. The paleness of the old bishop's skin and the serious expression on the doctor's face told Leviticus more than he wanted to know. A trembling raced down his spine. The doctor must have told Otto the worst before coming in to talk with Albert. Tough as he was, Otto kept taking in deep breaths, like he was having trouble holding in his heartbreak.

Leviticus observed his father. Was the shrunken, blue-skinned old man of *Gott* ready to hear what was coming? *How could he be?* No one was prepared for bad news, no matter what their age.

His gaze swept to Verity. She stood tall and straight, and altogether too lovely for the heartache about to be heaped on her. A nerve ticked in her cheek, proving she was seething with anger. Without a doubt, the strong Amish woman would put a stop to

Otto's wedding plans the first chance she got. She was no one's fool. Even he knew he wasn't good enough for her.

Solomon stepped forward, avoiding his brother's gaze. "Doctor Wendell?"

"Yes." She approached, her small-boned hand extended. "You must be Albert's youngest son, Leviticus. He's been asking for you."

Solomon's face blanched. With a scowl, he gestured his brother's way. "*Nee*. He'd be Leviticus."

"Doctor Wendell." Leviticus took the doctor's extended hand. Her grip was strong as any man's.

She glanced around, taking in the number of people in the small hospital room. "Perhaps I could have some privacy with you and your brother."

He looked at his father, waiting for a cue from him. Did he want everyone to know about the seriousness of his health? Albert lay still and quiet, his eyes opened and focused. Leviticus nodded. "We're all family here. You can speak freely."

Doctor Wendell directed her words to his father. "Our test results show you've recently had multiple ministrokes. There's also evidence of a past silent heart attack that's left one of your heart's ventricles slightly damaged."

He kept an eye on his father's facial expression as he took in her words. Optimism turned to resignation.

"I'm sorry, but we can't do bypass surgery on you. Your body's been weakened by undiagnosed type two diabetes and mild kidney failure, which we need to get under control before we make any further plans."

Solomon stood by their father's bed, his hand clutching Albert's. Leviticus thought he saw Verity sway, but she quickly righted herself.

He realized he'd been holding his breath and took in a raspy gulp of air. The room tilted. Tiny dots of light blurred his vision. *That's right, Sergeant. Faint at the foot of your father's bed.*

"I wish I had better news, Mr. Hilty, but

I've consulted with several of the on-staff cardiologists. We all agree. Perhaps in time, six months or more, we can operate, but for now we want you to heal and become stable."

His father's throat worked. *"Danki."* His word was as clear as a bell, as if nothing the doctor had said had touched his frail mind.

But the reality of the doctor's words hit Leviticus hard. He had to sit, concentrate on keeping his knees from knocking together as he trembled uncontrollably. He'd come home to rekindle his relationship with his father, only to lose him again? Anger welled up. He had no one to blame but himself. This was *Gott*'s will for Albert's life. His father seemed resigned to his fate, be it death or surgery somewhere down the road. Somehow, he had to learn to trust *Gott* in the same way.

Help me, Lord. Show my vadder *favor.*

Verity peddled as fast as she could, her dress and apron soaked and sticking to her from another heavy downfall of rain. She regretted not accepting Otto Fischer's offer of a ride home from Memorial Hospital, where Albert lay fighting for his life.

Otto had said Mose had room for her in the cab of his furniture truck and that her bike could be stored in the back until they got to the grove. But no. It wasn't raining then so she'd stubbornly refused, convinced she needed time to think.

With the back of her hand, she wiped rain from her eyes. *What a fool I am. I would be home already.*

Clara would have picked up the children from her mother's by now. Faith would be waiting for her, wondering where she was. At five, the little girl wasn't old enough to really understand the seriousness of Albert's illness.

Verity shoved a wet strand of hair out of her eyes and sped up. Like all humans, Albert would someday die. She knew that. The problem was, she loved the kind old man almost as much as she loved her own father and didn't want to lose him. Mixed in with her own emotions, she didn't want Albert to die for Leviticus's sake, as well, and the feeling made her frustrated. He'd left Pinecraft on his own. If he'd come home too late, it was on him, not her.

Grief and anger added power to her legs.

Am I mad at Gott*?* Shaken, she had to admit she was. She could lie to herself, but she wasn't fooling Him. The Father knew how she felt about Albert's poor health and the arranged marriage to Leviticus. She lowered her shoulders and sped on, almost blinded by the downpour. Sometimes life made no sense at all. *Gott* had taken Mark from her, as well as her tiny *soh.* Would Albert soon rest on that lonely hill on the grove where his wife lay?

She didn't bother to wipe the tears streaming down her face. The rain took away all traces of her anguish. She sniffed, stuffed down her bitterness and peddled on. Her damp skirt and the up-and-down motion of her knees made it hard to see eroding potholes in the unpaved road she had to travel back to the grove.

A vehicle honked behind her. Startled, she splashed through a deep pothole she normally would have seen and avoided. With a bump, she fell over.

Thanks to the rain pouring down in sheets, it took real effort to untangle herself from the bike and crawl to the edge of the road. Her knee hurt and her palm was bleeding.

She heard the vehicle door slam shut and looked up. *Probably the fool who honked and caused me to fall.*

A long-legged man walked over. "You all right?"

Ach. She didn't have to look up. She knew Leviticus's voice. Why did he have to drive past now? Couldn't it have been Ulla, or one of the other local *grossmammi* who often traveled down the lane to buy fruit from Albert or Solomon?

Thunder clapped overhead. A warning from *Gott* that He would not put up with any more of her pettiness about Leviticus?

She rose like a phoenix out of the ashes, until the toe of her shoe caught one of the spokes of the bike wheel and caused her to fall on her already bloodied knee. Muddy water splashed up in her face, momentarily blinding her.

"Here. Let me help."

Under his drenched hat, was that a smirk on Leviticus's face? No, but his tone sounded much too amused for her liking. She would have expected him to mock her situation when he'd been a *bu*, but today? Back then, they'd teased each other mercilessly, but they were grown now.

She peeked at her grazed knee. Her skin was dotted with ground-in bits of tiny gravel. It was sure to hurt after the thorough cleaning it needed.

Leviticus extended his hand toward her. His fingertips dripped with rain. She pondered her dilemma. Surely, the sin of pride wouldn't keep her sitting in a mud puddle? Anger and frustration warmed her face, but she reached out and accepted his firm grip.

She'd ride in the old truck with him, but that didn't mean she had to talk to him. She had nothing to say. Not a word. *Gott* kept reminding her that He, in His loving mercy, required her to forgive Leviticus for the past, but He'd said nothing about her having to like the man.

"I thought you got a ride home with Otto." Leviticus hoisted her into the truck's front seat with a grunt.

"*Nee*, I'd ridden my bike into town and couldn't just leave it at the hospital." *You're beginning to lie much too easily.* "It wasn't raining when I started off." At least that much was true. She avoided his gaze, seething inside. Ya, *I know,* Gott. *I must find my way out of this mess without harming my walk with You.*

Leviticus deposited her bike in the truck's rusty bed with ease, as if the ancient bike weighed less than nothing.

The driver's side door opened, and he dashed in and buckled his seat belt. Rain and mud dripped off them both, and onto his truck seats and floor mats. Her grumpy mood allowed a measure of satisfaction at the mess being made. Thoughts totally unworthy of a Plain woman.

Busy buckling up, she imagined how disappointed *Gott* must be in her, especially when Leviticus handed her a soft white handkerchief and said, “Press that against your knee. It’s clean.”

“Danki.” His kind act made her feel even more mean-spirited and worthy of *Gott*’s punishment. She sucked in her breath as the cloth touched her skin.

“If I were you, I’d clean that scrape really well when you get home.”

“I will.” Did he think her a *bensel*? She was a mother, after all. She’d become an expert at cleaning scrapes and bumps.

He’s been nothing but nice to you since he came home. Did her conscience always have to be right? Couldn’t she get away with one harsh thought without feeling petty?

“More rain is the last thing the grove needs.” Leviticus clicked on the windshield wipers, flipped on the truck's turn signal and roared off down the road.

Pinecraft had experienced many hurricanes, but this last one seemed far worse than the others to her. It had lingered over the tiny community, demonstrating a will of its own while destroying property and people's lives without apology or signs of remorse. What the main brunt of the wind and downpours hadn't decimated, the residual rain bands forecasted for the next few days would finish off.

Leviticus pulled into the drive and stopped close to the farmhouse. He turned off the engine and unbuckled his seat belt as his head turned toward Verity.

Dealing with daunting thoughts, Verity watched the windshield wipers slow and then come to a stop before she realized they'd arrived at the farm. She needed to get inside, wanted to get away from Leviticus more than she'd ever wanted anything. The man kept her in a maelstrom of self-pity and bitter, confused emotions. But before she could reach for the door handle, he stopped her with the touch of his hand on her arm. “Wait. Before you go in, I need to talk to you in private.”

Keeping her eyes straight ahead, she unpinned her drooping prayer *kapp* and laid it in her lap. “Our *dochders* haven’t seen us since yesterday. Perhaps another time would be better.”

He drew back his arm. “Give me five minutes, Verity. Please.”

With a swipe of her hand, she pushed strands of wet hair off her face before daring a glance Leviticus’s way. His hair was wet and plastered to his head like a pale skullcap. Holding his gaze, she was taken aback by the look of sincerity in his eyes. Her resolve to be distant and direct with him crumbled. It was early morning. Clara could handle Naomi’s feeding. Faith, most likely, was still asleep. “Five minutes,” she agreed and waited for his words.

“I know you’re upset by Otto’s crazy plan.”

“Upset? I think *revolted* is a far better

word. Why did you suggest there might be a chance we'd court again?" *There's no reason to be cruel.* "I'm sorry. That was mean-spirited of me and totally unnecessary." She lowered her head. "I wasn't prepared…didn't imagine you'd mention my name to Otto and that he'd come up with such nonsense as a marriage of convenience. Do he and Albert really expect us to marry without so much as a private conversation between the two of us? There have to be far better choices."

"He misunderstood what I was trying to say when I spoke your name. He's growing older. Don't blame Otto for the mistake. I should have made my intent clear. Remember, he only wants what he feels is best for us."

"*Ya*, well, if someone had bothered to ask me, I would have told them I have no plans to ever remarry." Verity pulled her wet skirt away from her stinging knee. She yearned for a long hot bath. Sweet-smelling shampoo.

I'm not going to marry Leviticus Hilty.

Not anyone. Period. If he needed a wife so badly, she could think of a half-dozen *maidals* and widows who were interested in marriage.

As if reading her thoughts, he spoke. "Otto wants *you* for my wife, plain and simple. If it makes you feel any better, I didn't have any say in the matter, either."

Verity could feel heat rising past her neck and into her cheeks. "And you? Am I not *gut* enough for you now that you've experienced the *Englischer* world?" Her fingernails cut into the palms of her hands. *Why did I say that?*

He rubbed the side of his nose. Remained silent. Finally, he spoke, his words coming slow. "I feel the same about marriage. I'm not ready, but it seems Otto's not going to accept any option but his own." He glanced her way. "But like you said, it won't work between us."

The words *why not?* almost came out of her mouth, but she stifled them and swallowed hard before she made another blunder.

The last thing she needed was him thinking she wanted to be his *fraa*, and a *mamm* for his *kind.* "You must know my decision not to marry has nothing to do with Naomi. She's a lovely *kind.* Any woman would be blessed to have her as their *boppli.*"

"Not every woman." His tone grew hard, his eyes narrowing. "Some women love their profession more than they love their own *kinner.*"

That haunted look was back in his eyes. An aching ball in the pit of her stomach told Verity she didn't dislike Leviticus quite as much as she thought. In that moment, she hurt for him. Hurt for tiny Naomi... But certainly not enough to make them her *familye.* She'd help him find a wife. Someone who could love him. But that was all she'd do.

She took in a deep breath and prayed for guidance silently. "I've been thinking. Your *daed* is fond of me. Perhaps he suggested to Otto that we wed. Albert knows you'll need someone to help you through the difficult times if he passes and wants to tie you down to the grove, so you'll stay. Solomon loves the land. But you? I don't think Albert's so sure you'll stay unless you have a good reason." She tipped her head down, concentrating on the mud chunks and splatter on her plain black shoes. She couldn't look him in the face and say harsh words. Not with that hound dog expression in his eyes. "I'm sorry, but I won't marry you, Leviticus. I—I can't."

"Perhaps we could pretend to court. The pretense doesn't have to end in marriage. Lots of couples end their relationships before their wedding dates."

She raised her head. "I'll simply tell Albert I'm not ready to remarry and he'll understand."

"Will he?" Leviticus's frown made him look as doubtful as she felt. "He didn't seem to be thinking too clearly today. The stroke's affected his mind. And as for Otto, he always gets his way. If I'm willing to sacrifice a short period of time for *Daed* and pretend, why can't you?"

Verity all but sputtered, her annoyance growing with each word out of his mouth. “You make it sound like spending time with me would be a sacrifice you’d have to endure. A bitter pill to swallow.”

“That’s not exactly what I meant.” He ran his hand through his pale wet hair, leaving plowed furrows.

“Not your exact words, but close enough.” Verity clasped the door handle. “I’m the hired help, the paid housekeeper, remember? Nothing more.” She opened the truck’s door. Rain blew in, drenching her again. “I’ll continue working until I’m no longer needed, and then Faith and I will leave.”

“Where will you go?” he called after her. “Back to your parents’ home just as they’re ready to retire?”

Yes, she would have to go home. And her going home would disrupt her parents’ future as they got older. They still had young *kinner* in an already crowded house. The reality of her situation didn’t sit well with her, making her reply sharp. “My future is my business, Leviticus. Not yours." She stepped out of the muddy truck. "Find yourself another sacrificial lamb!"

As she trudged toward the door, she dealt with reality. She had no choice but to obey the community's *Ordnung* rule of obedience to authority, and Otto certainly was her authority.

She hurried in, wanting to be away from Leviticus. A strong gust of wind caught the door as she stepped into the house, slamming it behind her, right in Leviticus's face. At least he couldn't blame her for the gesture. Or would he?

Chapter Eight

Leviticus swung the door open and hurried in, the wind-driven rain wetting the great room's wooden floor. He worked on checking his rising temper. Waves of anger rolled over him. He'd had a hard time dealing with drama of any kind since the war. The smallest things could set him off, cause him to lose his temper. *Be calm. Don't say more than is needed.*

He understood where Verity was coming from. He didn't blame her. Not really. He had no right to expect her to go along with a pretend engagement or unwanted wedding.

They were virtual strangers now, and marriage *was* forever for the Amish.

A troubling thought hit him. *Perhaps Verity has a reason for not wanting to court.* Did she already have someone she was fond of? But what difference did it make to him? He had no intentions of marrying, and certainly not Verity. He wasn't *gut* marriage material, and not fit for any woman for that matter. He was damaged goods. A life alone was what he deserved. But what about Naomi and her need for a *mamm*?

Wise up, Leviticus. Verity's a fine woman. Why wouldn't someone be interested in her by now? She's not for you. You gave up your chance long ago and now it's much too late.

He found Verity and an Amish teenage girl he didn't recognize standing by the table. Verity's expression had softened. Faith came running past him, her arms outstretched toward her mother. The child's blue eyes sparkled with joy. "*Mamm!* I thought you were gone forever."

Shut out, he watched as Verity knelt and

scooped up her daughter, holding her close to her heart. Her rain-soaked clothes saturated Faith's plain cotton nightdress, but the *kind* didn't complain or pull away. She held on to her mother for dear life.

"I'd never leave you, *liebling.* You know that. I was with Albert. He's sick again and needed me."

"I don't want him to go live with Jesus." Faith's lip trembled, her blue eyes were big, round and earnest.

"Who told you such a thing?" Verity glanced over her shoulder, her gaze resting on the gangly, freckled-faced teenager standing a few feet away.

"*Aenti* Irene came to help with Naomi. A minute ago, I heard her tell Clara that Albert might die." The little girl clung to her mother's neck. "Is it true?"

Saying nothing, Leviticus bent to remove his filthy boots at the back door.

"I'm sorry for my *schweschder*'s foolish words, Leviticus. She had no right speaking to anyone about your *daed*'s condition.

She's old enough to realize this kind of conversation is best left for adults."

"Faith would have overheard someone soon enough," he stated matter-of-factly. Death had become black-and-white to him since the war.

Verity laid her *kapp* on the kitchen table and adjusted her bun once again. "*Ya*, sure. She probably would have, but in the right way and at the right time, from me." Verity shot another accusing look at her sister, who ducked her head in shame.

"Is there a good time to learn of a loved one's impending death?" Leviticus padded across the room in his rain-soaked socks, past Verity and the red-faced teen who was a younger blond-haired version of Verity. His mind was trying to concentrate on things eternal. He needed to pray, ask God to touch his father before he lost him forever. And he needed to pray for himself, too. And for Solomon, his *familye* and the grove. As for the foolish arrangements made by Otto? They'd figure something out eventually. "I'll be in my room if you need me."

A headache beginning, he rubbed his temples as he moved down the dark hall toward his bedroom. His *mamm*'s sewing room door stood open and a young man came strolling out, whistling, his bright red hair and freckled nose a sure sign he was another of Verity's kin, perhaps her younger brother. The teen wore traditional Amish garb, but his coppery hair was shorter than most Amish boys'. *Enjoying* rumspringa, *no doubt.* "You're kin to Verity, if I remember correctly. Your name's Joel?" He took the *bu*'s extended hand and they exchanged firm handshakes.

"*Ya*, I'm Joel, Verity's youngest *bruder*. And you're Leviticus, Albert's youngest, too."

"I am."

Joel placed a battered baseball cap on his head and shoved up the brim. "Mom told me about your *daed*'s illness. I hope he gets better soon. Albert's a *gut mann*. I got to know him when he coached our baseball team when I was a young *bu*."

Leviticus nodded. There were so many things he didn't remember about his father. The man's love of sports was one of them. He shoved his shaking hands in his pockets and cleared his throat, his stomach roiling, his head pounding. "*Ya*, he's a fine man."

Joel nodded toward the door he'd stepped out of. "I hope you don't mind me using your mom's old sewing room as a bedroom. I moved in while you were in the grove this morning. *Mamm* said I'd only be staying for a couple of weeks, at the most."

Stuck in his own misery, Leviticus struggled to maintain coherent thought. "Staying?"

"*Mamm* said Verity needed a chaperone until the wedding, and since I'm still on walkabout, I got picked." A half grin played on Joel's face, revealing his boyish, playful side. "You know how *mamms* are. Always protecting their *kinner*."

Leviticus ignored Joel's reference to the

wedding that would never happen. Instead, he thought about his mother's smiling face. "Enjoy your *mamm* while you can, *soh*. They're precious and don't live forever."

"*Ya*, I know." Joel scratched his shoulder and stepped away. "I guess I should get out to the grove and help the men gather up as much of the rotting fruit as we can before nightfall." Joel patted Leviticus's upper arm in a brotherly fashion and said, "Don't worry too much. Albert's in *gut* hands."

Leviticus nodded his agreement. "Solomon's already home from the hospital?"

"He came in a few minutes ago and stayed just long enough to tell Clara their home repairs were almost complete and that they'd be moving back sooner than he'd thought. You want me to give him a message when I see him?"

Leviticus faked a smile. "That's okay. I'll catch up with him in a bit."

Joel lifted his hand in a friendly goodbye. "*Gut* meeting you. I'll tell your *bruder* you asked after him. You'll be coming out to help in a bit? Solomon's going to need every hand he can get."

"Ya," Leviticus answered, but wasn't sure if he'd go to the grove today. His mind was a mess and his head still pounded with a growing migraine. "Hey, thanks for coming over and giving us a hand. I know Solomon appreciates the help."

Joel smiled. "I'm glad to do what I can." His deep voice cracked as only a teenager's could, and then he walked away.

Leviticus slumped against the doorjamb, tired in spirit and mind. *I should go work in the fields, contribute something more than drama.* He puffed out a fatigued breath. Today or tomorrow, he had to deal with Solomon's remaining fury sometime. He needed to settle things between them before another encounter caused their father's death, and not just a debilitating stroke. *Give me time, Lord. And the right words.*

He opened his bedroom door and the years fell away. The room had become a time capsule, everything the same as when he'd left.

He fingered the wooden truck his brother, Solomon, had hand-whittled out of wood when he'd been only nine. They'd been close back then, done everything together like *bruders* should. But then he'd met the *Englischer* teens. They'd become his only friends just before eighth grade. He began to long for the things they bragged about. The big screen TVs and music videos. His rebellious attitude had eventually separated him from his *bruder*, who wanted nothing more than to be a good Amish *bu*.

Leviticus dropped his head, remembering how he'd become a disobedient loudmouth by the time he'd finished eighth grade and left school. He managed to make everyone around him miserable, especially Solomon. But Verity had fallen in love with him regardless.

Back then, Leviticus hadn't been sure he wanted to be Amish; he certainly hadn't wanted to obey the rules put in place for his own safekeeping. But his mother's sudden death shook him to his foundation, turned him against his father and his community and sealed his fate. He left broken and went to learn about the *Englischer* world. Like a fool, he'd gladly fought the *Englischers'* war, and ended up almost dying on their battlefield. Now he had to live with his messed-up head, the memories that made him want to throw up every time one of them flickered through his mind. For a time, it felt like death followed him around.

He pulled off his damp, soiled socks and lay back on his bed, his eyes closing, his head pressing into the softness of the pillow. Images of his father in the hospital bed followed him into his restless sleep, tormenting his mind.

Verity struggled to absorb the happenings of the day and failed miserably. She worked mechanically around the kitchen, wanting to keep herself busy so she wouldn't have time to think too deeply about what was going on around her.

White powdery puffs of flour rose to

tickle her nose as she dusted cut-up chicken after dipping each piece in egg batter. She worked blindly, not really seeing anything but Albert's expression as the doctor spoke of his possible demise. She knew him well. He'd tried to hide his shock from all of them, but she'd seen it.

Minutes later, she washed glops of flour and egg off her hands as her *mamm* carefully dropped the coated chicken into hot grease. "You think anyone's going to want to eat?"

Verity's mother moved Faith away to keep the chicken from popping hot fat on her. "People don't stop eating just because they're tired and their hearts are troubled. Solomon's been working in the field most of the day. Leviticus joined him a few hours ago. They'll both be tired and looking for a good hearty dinner."

Verity finished cleaning her hands and then dried them with a dishcloth. She smiled at her daughter coloring at the table and then turned back to her mother. Her attempt at a genuine smile felt feeble, at best.

"We're all grieving Albert's diagnosis. You're not the only one who loves him." Her mother put a generous dab of butter into a pot of fresh, steaming green beans.

Verity nodded. "I know." She'd always had a good relationship with her *mamm*, even when she'd been a teen and as rebellious and mouthy as they came. When Leviticus had left her high and dry and her heart felt broken, it was her mother who soothed her, got her back on track, helped her find Mark, the one man who had truly loved her.

Memories of Mark, his dark hair, the way he showed his love for life when he smiled, moved her to tears. He'd been a *gut* husband and she couldn't even remember the sound of his voice anymore. She longed to hear him say he loved her just one more time.

She stared at her *mamm*'s back as the older woman took plates down from the cupboard. She couldn't imagine the pain that would come with losing one of her parents. She brushed away tears and stirred the creamed corn, her thoughts dark and broody from the day's events.

She could tell Leviticus had been devastated by the doctor's news. There was hope, but having so many sudden strokes could take him in a week or a year from now.

Leviticus had returned after a long spell away to be close to his *daed*. Stepping in his shoes for a moment, her heart became pained, as if a mule had kicked her in the chest. She could only imagine what he was going through, and she'd done so little to make things easier for him.

In a fog of regret, she mindlessly cut potatoes into wedges, placed them on a flat roasting pan, drizzled them with oil, salt and pepper, and put them in the hot oven to bake. "Otto wants me to marry Leviticus." Her words slipped out in a whisper so that Faith wouldn't hear.

"I know." Her *mamm*'s head bobbed as she placed a bowl on the counter and then pulled Verity into the privacy of the food pantry. "Your *daed* and I talked about the arrangement last night and can see wisdom in Otto's plan. Leviticus needs the love of a *gut* woman, someone to teach him how to be Amish again. You've been alone far too long and lonely. I see it in your eyes." She caught her daughter's hand. "You've become headstrong and bitter. Set in your ways." She glanced into the kitchen where Faith continued her coloring. "You have Faith's needs to consider, too."

Her *mamm* continued talking in the semidarkness, unaware that Verity stood transfixed like a wooden statue, her mouth open like a baby bird seeking food from its mother's beak.

"Faith needs a *schweschder* or *bruder*, and since Leviticus already has a *kind* of his own, your sweet *kind* won't have to wait long for that *schweschder* she keeps asking for. *Gott* will bless you and Leviticus with *kinner* of your own eventually." Releasing her hand, her *mamm* picked up a jar of pickles and one of olives, her mouth stretched

which was little more than an inch taller than Verity. Her brows lowered, disapproval in her expression. "When did you become so hard, *dochder*? *Ya*, Leviticus left you and the community behind, abandoned his *familye*, but he has seen the error of his ways and returned to his roots, to the faith he was meant to embrace. He had not joined the church before he left, but Otto tells me Leviticus has asked for forgiveness and now seeks redemption from *Gott* in membership and baptism. What more do you require to forgive? Are your wants and needs more important than *Gott*'s will for your life?"

Her countenance softening, her *mamm* took Verity's hand again and whispered, "What would Mark think of this judgmental attitude you carry round like a yoke on your neck? The faithful have voted. Otto's given his approval. Leviticus will be allowed to join the church come Sunday service, and will get baptized that afternoon, as all good Amish men do once they come to a spiritual understanding with *Gott*. Are you so high and mighty that you see yourself as better than Leviticus? Is there no way that he can prove himself worthy of your love? Did I raise a woman who is proud, or are you hiding behind bruised feelings?"

Her *mamm*'s words cut into her soul and condemned her. Was she too proud to accept the bishop's plan? Was she being prideful, arrogant and haughty? She was repulsed by the thought. She had become *hochmut*.

She'd sought after the *demut* and *gelassenheit* all her adult life, and longed to be full of humility, composure and placidity. Did self-will hold her back, or was she resisting the arranged marriage because, deep down, it *was* what she really wanted? Could it be possible she was ashamed that she still had feelings left for Leviticus Hilty after he abandoned her?

"I'll consider your words and pray on this, *Mamm*. It's the best I can do. I'm sorry if I've disappointed you."

"Be more concerned how *Gott* feels about your expressions of distaste for one of His own *kinner*, Verity. *Gott* loves us all, both good and bad. He has a plan and we all must seek His will and be satisfied."

Verity accepted a warm hug from her *mamm* and wiped at the tears dampening her eyes.

"I wouldn't ask something of you that wouldn't benefit you, my *liebling*. I know the real you would gladly follow *Gott*'s direction, and our community's *Ordnung*. I believe this arrangement is *Gott*'s will for your life. Embrace it. Seek *Gott*'s face before you reject Leviticus, this marriage of convenience. Don't make a fool of yourself and go your own way. That's what Leviticus did. There's evil in this world and danger in that kind of thinking."

Verity drew in a deep breath. "I'm willing to ask *Gott* for His will in my life." *But can I?* Could she dedicate her whole life to the man who'd walked away from her? Was this sacrifice too much to ask of her, or was she being stiff-necked and hardheaded?

"I know you love me and believe this marriage to Leviticus will bring Faith and me happiness." *Only time will tell if* Mamm *is right.* "Leviticus left for the grove hours ago, but first chance I get, I'll talk to him. But only after I pray."

Chapter Nine

Thick pork chops sizzled in the big frying pan and a cheesy casserole bubbled in the oven, ready for the noon meal. At the counter, Verity prepared fresh vegetables for a garden salad. Her eyes intermittently checked on the girls as they played across the room with a pile of pots and pans.

Shy when she'd first come to the grove, there was no holding Naomi back now, and with Faith's encouragement, the toddler was able to express herself with sentences of gibberish and lots of toothy grins.

Leviticus walked in the back door, his hand at his back as he squatted to greet his daughter first and then Faith. “So what kind of morning have you two had? I got to play in the mud all day. You would have loved the mess, Faith.”

Faith took the time to hug Leviticus’s neck, but was quickly back to “making dinner” with Naomi, who was busy sucking on a pot lid. “My *mamm* doesn’t let me play in mud. She gets angry. Were you allowed to play in the mud when you were little?”

Verity sucked in her breath and held it, waiting for Leviticus to reply. He didn’t like talking about his mother with her, or anyone else as far as she knew. In fact, she hadn’t heard him mention his mother once since he’d been home.

“You can be certain-sure my *mamm* got mad, but she got over it quick enough. Kind of like your *mamm* does.” He glanced up at Verity and smiled a tired smile, his lip barely inching up. They hadn’t spoken more than a half-dozen words since they’d talked about a marriage of convenience. Naomi crawled over to her father and used handfuls of his shirt for support as she lifted herself on bowed legs and took tentative tiptoe steps around him. *"Dat, dat, dat,"* she chimed, her grin wide, expressing her love for the man covered in dry sandy loam.

"That's right. I'm your *dat*." Leviticus's face beamed. He lifted his gaze from his *dochder* and then centered it on Verity as he said, "She'll be walking soon. Ain't so?"

Verity placed the cooked chops on a platter and covered the golden-brown meat with foil. The cheesy casserole needed a bit more browning and then they'd be able to sit down for lunch. She found herself grinning like a silly fool, her pride in Naomi's accomplishments overwhelming her. "I'm already finding her walking around the couch and anything else she can pull up on." She patted sweat from her forehead on the sleeve of her dress and went back to dicing carrots.

"I'm filthy and ruining your clean floors. Do I have time for a quick shower?" Leviticus chucked first Faith and then Naomi under the chin and had them giggling in no time.

Verity nodded, avoiding looking at him as he left the room. She hid the flush on her face that had nothing to do with the heat of the kitchen. She couldn't help but notice how much of a *familye* they were becoming, each of them settling in their role as if it was the most natural thing in the world to do. *This is what it would have been like if Leviticus had stayed, and we'd married all those years ago.* Hard work, *kinner* and love, but the love was missing from this *familye* unit, save the *kinner*'s affection for them both. If they married, would the love ever return? Could she love him again the way she had as a girl, with all her heart and soul? "I'll get the *kinner*'s food."

Once she had Naomi in her high chair and Faith in her chair, the girls paused for prayer and began to eat without protest. It had been a long time since breakfast and they'd played hard all morning.

Verity prepared a warmed plate for Leviticus while keeping an eye on Naomi as the toddler made fast work of her bowl of cubed, cooked carrots. Verity had just set his plate on the table when Leviticus walked back in the kitchen, his hair damp and ruffled.

In his haste, he'd left his suspenders hanging at his sides like he used to do as a *bu*. Memories rushed in. Leviticus had told her he hated suspenders back then, and she wondered if he was any fonder of them now. Some things never changed. Just their love.

She took in a deep breath and pretended they had no past, that her heart hadn't been broken beyond repair by the man pulling out a chair and joining her for their noon meal.

Verity sat between the girls as she usually did, directly across from Leviticus. Together they bowed their heads in silent prayer. Leviticus lifted his head a moment later, his gaze catching hers. There was a look in his eyes, something unreadable, but she dared a guess he was thinking about the grove, all the work still left to do. She took a bite of pork and chewed, appreciating the tangy flavor of ginger. “Mmm, this pork is tender.”

Leviticus nodded, even though he hadn’t taken a bite of food. Much like Faith did when she wasn’t hungry, he pushed his food around with his fork.

“I caught a butterfly today.” Faith poked a chunk of meat in her mouth and spoke around it. “*Mamm* said it was the prettiest she ever saw.”

Leviticus looked up. “I’m sure it was pretty, sweet girl.” He smiled. “When I was a *bu* I used to catch butterflies and put them in a jar, but my *mamm* would find them in my bedroom and make me let them go. She said I was being mean by keeping them from their families in her rose garden.”

Faith swallowed her meat and speared another piece. “Can your *mamm* come visit us sometime? She sounds nice.”

Leviticus shoved his plate away and rose from the table. “*Nee, liebling.* My *mamm* went to live with Jesus a long time ago. Long before you were born.”

"I'm sorry," Faith murmured, her eyes wide. "I'd miss my *mamm* if she went away."

"I'd miss your *mamm*, too," Leviticus answered, and moved toward the door. "I'm going back out to the grove. There's a lot of work to be done."

"*Ya*, sure." Verity looked down at Leviticus's abandoned plate as the back door slammed. He hadn't eaten a thing. He needed nourishment for all the hard work he was doing, but he ate less than Albert did on a good day.

Had Faith's conversation about his *mamm* run him off? She never knew for sure what would upset him anymore. He'd changed, become more sensitive, hard to read.

Lord, help me to help him. I don't want to wed him, but I hate seeing him so unhappy. Like he doesn't have a friend to call his own.

Her own appetite gone, she cleared the table, wiped down the girls and sent them off to play at her feet as she washed the dishes. So much was going on. She couldn't keep her emotions steady. She looked at the girls, her heart swelling. One thing her mother was right about—these *kinner* needed both a *mamm* and a *dat*. *Gut*, loving parents was *Gott*'s plan for a *kind*'s life. They were to be raised in a home full of love. But there was no love between her and Leviticus. Wouldn't they be cheating the girls out of a loving environment if they married?

Leviticus was still gone as darkness shrouded the house and groves. Solomon left for the hospital, leaving Clara behind to help finish the supper dishes. Glad Clara and Solomon were still living in the house, Verity smiled as she bathed Naomi and fed her a bottle before bed. After a kiss on her head, she hummed low and sweet, her hand soothing the restless toddler with circular motions on her back. She chose to hum one of Faith's favorite songs, all the while thinking, *Where has Leviticus gone?*

Naomi soon fell asleep, her thumb stuck in her rosebud mouth, but Faith was another matter altogether. Just keeping her in bed was a nightly battle. The child needed a firm hand, a father to stand his ground and show her he meant business.

Minutes later, stars sparkled as Verity stepped out onto the porch. A fall moon hung heavy in the clear night sky, its beauty there for everyone willing to raise his or her head. Verity stepped farther into night, her old cotton dress glistening in the moonlight. She slipped into her favorite chair, the one Leviticus had made for his *mamm* before he'd escaped into the *Englischer* world.

She covered her bare feet and legs with the hand-crocheted throw Albert's *fraa* had made years ago. Tired, she eased back, her sigh soft. Why did life have to be so complicated?

Verity remained stationed in the rocker, thinking about Faith's need of a father. Since her daughter had been tiny, she'd fought bedtime. If only Mark were here to set down the law to the cranky little girl… But he wasn't. An ache tore through her. And he never would be again.

Through tears, she pushed away her pain and noticed the moon's glow shimmering on the rim of her tea mug. She lifted the drink and took a long, satisfying sip of the warm brew, then placed the mug on the arm of the wooden chair. She nestled back against the cushion, making another effort to get comfortable. She needed a bit of "me time," a moment to gather her thoughts and pray before she went to bed. Too much had gone on the last few days. Albert was better, but still ill. She and Leviticus's arranged marriage still hung in the air like a drifting black spider web ready to snare her.

Verity sucked in a long, calming breath, determined to find a measure of peace from the near-silent night. Moonlight pooled around her, placing her in a protective cocoon that would bring about a much-needed calm.

Her lashes dipped. She'd been up since five o'clock that morning. Naomi had woken her with the need of a clean diaper and warm milk. Her day had dragged on from there. There'd been so much drama since Leviticus's return and Albert's stroke. How long had it been since she'd slept through the night? She couldn't remember. Her normally calm nerves were stretched taut, almost to the point of breaking. Verity welcomed the solitude around her, the delicate sounds of the night creatures singing their lonely songs.

Earlier in the morning, her mother had come by the grove, inquiring about Albert and playing with the children while Verity washed tiny play clothes and a dress or two of her own. Her mother showing up had proven to be a blessing, but still Verity was glad when her mother had gone home to fix a meal for her own family.

Joel remained, still left behind to act as chaperone. Deep inside, she knew it was right he stayed. The *Ordnung* was clear. Single men and women did not share the same dwelling alone, and they would soon have to. Solomon was determined to dwell in his own home as soon as the damages from the storm were repaired.

A chill went through her. Thoughts of their proposed marriage sped up her already racing mind. She'd been hurt when he'd walked away from his life in Pinecraft. Walked away from her. Rejecting him came naturally to her, but somehow she couldn't honestly say she'd completely forgotten the love she'd once felt for him.

But if she'd wanted to remarry, she would have chosen a kind man of strong faith, someone older, who would make a good father for Faith. Someone completely opposite of Leviticus. Never would she have chosen a struggling *Englischer* who had to learn all over again what it meant to be Plain.

As if summoned up by her troubled thoughts, Leviticus pulled into the drive and the motor died. He ambled across the moonlit yard and up the stairs, his movements slow and easy. Was it her imagination or was he favoring his right leg a bit?

"You look comfortable." He sauntered

past, making his way toward the closed screen door.

"I was." Her reply was out before she had time to correct herself. *That's right. Pick on the man while his* daed *lies sick in the hospital.* There had to be a way to curb her anger besides cutting out her own tongue.

Since a child, she'd been taught to be humble. Not act like some spitfire with a chip on her shoulder. But here she was, thinking bitter thoughts and speaking harshly again.

She pulled forward and rolled the taut muscles in her neck and shoulders. Her mother's words came back to haunt her. She and Leviticus needed to talk, find a way to deal with this marriage situation once and for all.

"I'm sorry I disturbed you. I'll leave you to your peace and go look in on the girls." Leviticus's hand reached for the doorknob.

"*Nee*, wait. Don't go in just yet. Please." Gott, *You will have to put words in my mouth, because I don't have a clue what to say.* "We need to talk."

He remained silent but pulled a chair over and positioned himself next to her. He sat, his long legs stretched out in front of him, the dirty jeans he wore reminding her of who he still was. An *Englisch* man pretending to be Amish.

She swallowed hard. Even though her throat had gone dry, she began. "Did you see your *daed* tonight?" Her gaze drifted his way, but only for a moment. She wished she had time to figure out what to say. Forgiveness was required, and she had little to offer him. She could never marry him feeling this resentment.

She glanced back his way. He looked thin and restless, like he used to when he was young. His fingers tapped out a rhythm only he heard on the fabric of his jeans stretched across his thigh. All the changes in his life, his father's poor health had to be getting to him.

"*Ya*, I saw *Daed* earlier." He glanced up at the full moon and studied it like he'd just noticed its beauty. His face glowed, bathed in its light.

She nodded, even though he wasn't looking her way. She felt a need to acknowledge his words. Hope rose in her. Maybe Albert was thinking clearer now and realized what a foolish plan Otto had conjured up. "How does Albert look? Is he able to speak?"

"*Nee*, not much. Just a few words and they were almost unintelligible, but he looks better." He rubbed his hands up and down his arms, then massaged the muscles around his shoulder. "The nurse said this stroke did more damage than the last one, but his test results are improving a bit."

Verity finished her lukewarm tea, her eyes watching him over the rim of her cup. She found it impossible not to feel compassion for him, no matter how annoyed she was with him.

He turned toward her, as if he felt her eyes on him. He spoke casually. "Solomon came to see *Daed* just after I got there."

A cold breeze blew, ruffling the wispy hair

at the side of her cleaning scarf. "Have you two been able to get past your differences? You know you're going to have to find a way to mend old fences." She smoothed out the throw across her legs. She didn't want to talk too much about Albert. If she did, she would cry, and she refused to cry in front of him. "Albert's going to need both of his *sohs*."

His blue-eyed gaze sought her gaze. "I know, but *Daed*'s heart problems have Solomon running scared. He's angry, and not prepared to deal with me coming home, bringing shame to the *familye* again, and I can't blame him."

"You didn't tell your *daed* what I said to you, did you?" Verity's fingers picked at the twisted yarn that made up the crocheted throw on her lap.

"About you not wanting to marry me?" He settled back, his legs crossing at his ankles. "*Nee.* I didn't bring up the subject. It would just upset him. Come with me tomorrow and see *Daed*. We'll tell him our feelings together."

"We'll see," she murmured, the butterflies in her stomach fluttering. "I spoke with my *mudder*. About our marriage." She had to force her words out past raw nerves. She could have talked to young Leviticus about anything, but not this *Englischer* man. But they both had aged, changed. They were little more than strangers now. She tried to calm the pounding of her heart, but to no avail. As an Amish widow, she was expected to consider marriage offers after a suitable time and eventually marry but wouldn't be forced.

His laugh surprised her. It came out in a low rumble from deep inside his throat.

"I would have loved to have been a fly on the wall for that conversation." He leaned forward and looked directly at her. "What did she do? Threaten to take you home?" He laughed again. "She must think Otto's lost his mind…trying to match the two of us in holy matrimony."

She pulled up a strand of yarn from the throw and twisted it around her finger. He was the last person she wanted to admit this to, but it needed to be said. "She surprised me. She agrees with Otto. Said she and *Daed* think it's time I remarry. Seems I'm getting stodgy and set in my ways...like some *maidal*." She nibbled the edge of her lip, wishing she hadn't added the last part. She wasn't an old maid. She was a widow in mourning.

He pulled up his legs and twisted his chair around to face her. "Have you gotten stodgy?" he asked, a teasing tone entering his voice.

The flutter was back in her stomach, the moonlight and shadows cutting across his face, making him seem more appealing than she was comfortable with. "You don't want to know what I am." She tucked a wayward strand of hair in her scarf and continued. "But I'll tell you what I've decided to do."

He pulled off his baseball cap and laid it

in his lap, his hand running through his fair hair. "Go on."

There's no turning back now. You opened this can of worms. "I will promise to court you, pretend to love you, but that's all for now." She sucked in air and pressed on. Watching him for his reaction, she slumped back against the cushion like all the stuffing had been pulled out of her when he grinned, his dimple reappearing. That confounded dimple melted her insides, brought about a longing in her she could never understand, even as a young girl.

"Your promise is good enough for me."

Moonlight glistened on his fair hair as he spoke, making him look wan and ethereal.

Verity sank deeper in the chair. She recognized his satisfied smirk. She remembered it from a long time ago. He'd gotten his way again and he knew it. Her eyes burned from held-back tears of frustration. She jumped up, her bare feet smacking against the porch as she made a beeline for the door. "I've got to go check on the girls."

She didn't wait for his reply. She didn't have time to listen to his smug retort. Tears splashed down her face and onto the front of her dress as the screen door slammed behind her. She hurried to her room, her heart pounding in her ears. She didn't have the energy to deal with Leviticus anymore tonight.

Chapter Ten

An early chill from the north spread down the Florida peninsula during the night. Verity was going into town to talk to Albert privately, before the lies began. The last thing she wanted was to court a man she didn't love.

Perched on her bike, Verity ignored the light drizzle falling. She waved to Clara and Faith, who stood under the covering of the porch. The picture of disappointment, Faith clutched Clara's skirt.

"Don't worry. She's just disappointed she can't go with you, but she'll get over it. Right, Faith?"

Faith nodded, an impish grin replacing her sulky frown.

Verity appreciated Clara understanding her predicament. "*Danki* for helping out the last few days."

Clara grinned. "You can return the gesture when the *boppli* comes."

"You have a deal." Verity inspected the darkening skies overhead. "I'd best get going. This drizzle is turning into rain." She gave one last wave and pushed off, ignoring the cool breeze blowing at her back as she headed down the lane toward town. In a hurry, her legs pumped up and down, the graveled private road slick under her narrow bike wheels.

Leviticus would be returning from the grove soon, prepared to take her to see Albert. She didn't want to ride with him. She needed a chance to talk privately to his *daed*, without Leviticus there. It was her only hope to end this ruse before things got out of hand. Albert would listen. *He must.*

Thunder rumbled at a distance. Her heart

sank as she saw Leviticus's old truck turn down the grove's private lane. *When had he left that morning?* She hadn't heard him rumble past her bedroom window. It had to have been while she was bathing the *kinner.*

She dropped her head, peddling harder. The dark head covering and jacket she'd donned before leaving the house helped keep the rain off, and did a good job hiding her identity, too. Still, his truck slowed and came to a stop directly across from her.

As if she hadn't noticed him, she sped on, her bike tires slipping on the gravel from her sudden burst of speed. Rain pelted down, wetting the collar of her dress, dampening her hands and arms.

The truck reversed. Leviticus positioned himself alongside her. "Verity!" he called out through his partially opened truck window.

Her shoulders fell. She slowed to a stop, straddling the bike, her feet sinking into the gravel and mire. "I'll be back soon. I have a few things to do in town. Don't worry about

Naomi. My sister Rose is caring for her, and Clara is there!" she shouted over the racket his old truck's motor was making.

"It's not Naomi I'm worried about. It's you."

"Me?" she questioned, her thumb jerking toward her chest. "Why in the world are you worried about me?" She had to look like a fool, straddling a bike in the middle of a downpour. "I'm perfectly fine." Her words were a lie. She wasn't perfectly fine. She'd always been afraid of lightning and Leviticus knew it. She worked hard at not squirming as rain ran in rivulets down her back, dampening her dress.

"Yeah. I can see how fine you are." His dimple flashed her way, even though rain hit him full in the face. "Let me throw that bike in the back and I'll take you where you need to go."

Rain dripped off the end of her nose. "*Nee*, that's all right. I've only got a short way to travel. But *danki* for your kindness."

"Do we have to go through this again? Just get in."

"*Nee*, seriously. I'm fine." She pushed off, but thunder rumbled overhead again. Her fear of lightning stalled her.

"You're being ridiculous, you know." His teasing tone set her teeth on edge.

Lightning split the sky, illuminating her as thunder growled overhead. "I'm sure—"

He opened his door, lifted her off the bike as effortlessly as he might have Faith and moved around to the back of the truck.

Her back plastered to his chest, she tried to protest. His feet crunched against the wet gravel. He ignored her objections like he would a sullen child. She spat rain from her mouth, her protests silenced by the downpour.

He stopped next to the passenger side door and lowered her to her feet. His hands free, he opened the truck door and gave her an encouraging prod forward.

Furious at being manhandled, at his arrogance and condescending comments, she whirled on him and instantly wished she hadn't. He hadn't stepped back, and now her face was planted in the center of his hard chest. He smelled of rain, damp fabric and good plain Amish soap. Her knees went weak. She lifted her gaze. Leviticus's eyebrow arched, his expression as frustrated as she was feeling. Was this to be her plight with him, constantly needing his help and him driving her home like a runaway *kind*?

Verity sighed. *Just get in the truck. Don't make yourself look more foolish than you already do.*

"I'm not kidnapping you, you know. I'm just trying to get you out of the storm."

She watched him walk away, pick up her bike and place it in the back. Oh, how she hated it when he was right. She was still being hardheaded and churlish with him, and she knew it. A nasty storm was brewing overhead. She had no business trying to make it into town on a metal bicycle.

She clambered into the truck, arranged her damp, limp skirt around her legs and then took the dry cloth he handed her from the glove compartment. *"Danki."* She patted at her face and then jerked off her waterlogged head covering. Her prayer *kapp* came away with it. The tight bun she'd placed at the nape of her neck that morning unraveled, the coil of sodden hair falling against her back before she could gather it up.

She reached to grab the hair, but he brushed her hands away, exposing the ginger mane few eyes had seen loose around her shoulders. His gaze shifted to her face. "I've always loved your hair. It's the color of a new penny."

"*Ya*, well, it's a shame you never learned to love the whole of me." She jerked away. With little regard for her tender scalp, her fingers worked at twisting a bun back into place on her damp neck. She used her one and only remaining pin to secure the knot. In haste, she positioned her *kapp* and tied the wet ribbon under her damp neck.

He turned away from her. "I did love you, you know."

She didn't believe a word of it. "You picked a strange way of showing it, leaving the way you did." Her words were barely audible.

Their eyes met and held for a long moment. "I had my reasons for leaving." He dropped his chin.

"I'm sure you did, but did you stop to think your father might need you? Your *mamm*, his *fraa* of many years, had just passed. All he had left were you and Solomon." *Did you consider I might have needed you, too?*

He thrust the key in the ignition and the truck roared back to life. "I'm not going to pretend that what I did was right. At the time, I didn't think about anyone but myself and the pain of losing my *mamm*. I was selfish. I know that now. I don't need to be reminded." He impatiently swiped rain off his forehead. His eyes closed for a moment. "Look. I admit I wanted to join the *Englisch* world. See what it was like before I settled down. I lived one day at a time, until I looked around and years had passed. After a while I thought I'd been gone too long to return and be welcomed."

Her words were whispered, barely heard over the roar of the motor and pounding rain. "What finally brought you back?"

"Naomi." He took off down the rutted road with a spray of gravel.

Bouncing along beside him, Verity wished he'd said *you*, but he hadn't. She noticed how white his knuckles were on the steering wheel. The young *mann* who'd left her standing, waiting for him all those years ago, never would have admitted he'd made a mistake, even a small one. He'd been too proud. He would have bluffed his way through, made excuses. Maybe he'd changed, but had he changed enough?

And maybe he's working you, like he used to work his mamm.

The truck had barely come to a stop when Verity jumped out and hurried out into the rain while holding up her skirt. She rushed in through the back door without a glance back.

Leviticus parked under a mossy oak tree and slammed the truck door behind him. He hadn't made a mistake coming home. He wanted his *dochder* to know his family, the grove, the Amish way of life. Time had brought about change, but he still resented how hard his mother had seemed to work. Certain-sure his foolishness and too little rest had killed her. The responsibility for her being overworked, he laid at his *daed*'s feet.

The heavy rain bans on the edge of the retreating hurricane had left the ground soaked under his boots. He sloshed his way to the front yard, his mind whirling. Women liked choices, not mandates, even if they were Amish, like Verity, and raised to be subject to men's authority. He didn't have to be a mind reader to know she didn't want to marry him any more than he wanted to marry her, but he had a feeling she'd be fine being Naomi's mom…if he wasn't part of the deal. He could tell by the way Verity handled the child, especially when she thought no one was watching, that she loved Naomi.

He'd seen the tiny kisses she'd placed on the child's cheeks. Somehow, he had to convince Otto to rethink his plan of them marrying. He wasn't ready for two *kinner*, and he sure wasn't fit to be a husband.

He trod through the rain, trying his best to ignore the lightning and endure the sudden bursts of thunder so reminiscent of the IEDs blowing up around him during the war. Sudden noises set off memories of bomb attacks in the dark Afghan nights. One thing the army doctors had taught him was to face his issues head-on, not delay the inevitable. It was time he and Verity talked, got everything out in the open about his tour overseas. About Julie.

He shut the old farmhouse door quietly behind him. The great room was empty, but he could hear Faith's excited squeals coming from the kitchen and Naomi's urgent cry for milk. He hadn't taken time to feed her or share a smile with the rosy-cheeked child all day. Guilt ate at him, reminding him why he questioned his ability to be a good father.

Did he have what it took to bring up Naomi as Amish?

The kitchen door burst open, its hinges protesting as they announced Faith coming into the room. She wore a tiny dress of pale yellow, her shiny hair pulled back in a fly-away bun the size of a donut. She wore no prayer *kapp*; rather, it was clutched in her small hand. Her eyes were bright with excitement. She scurried over, her smile infectious. "Hello."

He found himself smiling back. "How are you, little one?"

She sidled up to him, almost touching. "My *mamm* said I'm not to bother you." Faith clutched her faceless doll under her arm. Mischievousness danced in her blue eyes. She plopped down on the floor, in front of the couch set back against the large picture window and cozied her doll among several square pillows. A square throw quilt, probably knitted by Verity, was draped casually across the doll's legs.

Apart from Naomi, he had little experience with children like Faith. He didn't know what to say, or what not to, but did his best to show she could trust him. "Did you have fun with Clara today?" He sat on the couch and saw the protective glance Faith gave her doll next to his leg. She didn't trust him fully, but he prayed she would in time.

Faith took her doll out from under the blanket and bounced it along the edge of the worn couch arm. "We made cupcakes. I ate two, but don't tell *Mamm*. She says I eat too much sugar."

In a surprise move, she opened her mouth wide and flashed tiny square molars. "Do you see any cavities? If I get one, *Mamm* says I have to visit the *Englischer* dentist again." She batted her ginger lashes at him. "Does it hurt to have a filling? *Mamm* said it could. Have you had a tooth filled?"

Leviticus wasn't sure which question to answer first. He wasn't about to admit he'd often canceled dental appointments until extreme pain had him reaching for the phone. He had to set a good example for Faith and

Naomi now. "I've seen the dentist lots of times. Brushing your teeth really good after eating sugar is the key."

"Your shirt is wet." She changed the subject. "Did it hurt?"

"What?" he asked, bemused. Like Verity, Faith had a way of delighting him, but kept him off-kilter with her rapid-fire way of talking.

Faith snickered. "The fillings? Did they hurt?" Her expectant gaze held his.

Hurt? Yes, it hurt. But a lot of things hurt in life.

He pulled his thoughts away from his problems, brought them back to the present, to Faith and the room they were in. Would his lack of concentration ever go away?

"Did it?" Faith asked again, her hands on her hips, waiting.

"Yes, sometimes it hurt, but just a bit. You look like a brave girl to me."

Faith looked guilty as Verity came into the room and took her by the hand, her forehead furrowed. "I told you not to bother Leviticus. He has a lot on his mind. Let's go see if we can help Clara fix a meal."

"You look brave to me," Faith called over her shoulder to Leviticus. Her skinny legs skipped alongside her mother, who flashed him a puzzled glance.

Leviticus watched as they disappeared down the hall. His chin dropped to his chest. *Brave. Ha!* If the little girl only knew what a coward he'd been in the war. He rose and moved toward his room, only to pause as his cell phone went off. "Hello."

The voice on the phone was formal and hurried. "Mr. Hilty. This is Janet Gaynor, your father's nurse. I'm afraid he's taken a turn for the worse. It's time you and the family get up here."

His vocal cords froze. He finally got out, "*Ya*, we'll be right there." His whole body went numb, his hand trembling so hard he almost dropped the cell phone.

"Oh, yes. Your brother said to bring Verity with you."

His brow creased in a deep V. He cleared

his voice. "You sure he didn't say to bring Clara, his wife?"

"No. He didn't mention anyone named Clara. I distinctly remember him saying the name Verity."

"Okay." His heart pounded, almost deafening him. "We'll be right there." He ended the call and looked around the room, confusion clouding his mind. Why would Solomon want Verity to come? She was close to his father, but not family, not like Clara was.

He shoved his cell phone back in his pocket and tried to walk, but his legs failed to cooperate. He called out to Verity from where he stood, his voice strained. Was his father dying? On a shelf, the light overhead sent a spark of reflection flickering off his mother's favorite jug. He drew in a deep breath, remembering how strong she'd been as she lay dying and drew strength from her memory. He made another attempt to move and found himself able to hurry down the hall toward the kitchen. Time was wasting.

As he opened the kitchen door, Faith scurried past, her laughter filled with mischief, Verity following close behind the giggling child. Naomi took tiny steps while holding on to Verity's hands. As Naomi passed on tiptoe, she glanced up at her *daed*, her expression decidedly anxious, like being up on her feet made her feel unsure.

"I need to talk to you," he told Verity, his joy at seeing Naomi's first tentative steps pushed back by overwhelming fear of what they'd find at the hospital.

Something in his tone must have gotten Verity's attention. She slowed and then stopped to lift Naomi to her hip. Her gaze searched his face. "What's wrong?" She moved back toward him, her smile slipping.

"It's *Daed.* The nurse—" His voice broke, but he struggled on. "She said to come now."

She nodded. "Go. Quick. Don't worry about Naomi. I will take *gut* care of her." Wiping a tear from her cheek, Verity turned to follow Faith.

"No. Wait. You don't understand. You

need to come. Clara will have to care for the *kinner.*"

"But why? Clara should be going with you. Solomon will want her there with him." Verity repositioned Naomi on her hip, her hands holding on to the squirming *kind.*

"I have no idea why Solomon said to bring you, but he did. The nurse said to come now. There was no time for questions. You're needed."

"But—"

"Look, if you don't want to come, just say so."

She shook her head. Her face had gone pale. "*Nee*, it's not that. I just don't understand."

He finally noticed the tick of nerves in her jaw, saw fear in her eyes and became gentle. "We'll figure it out later, Verity, but for right now, let's get the kids situated and hit the road."

Chapter Eleven

Verity's stomach roiled as she stared at the elevator. Until recently, she hadn't ridden in many and had hoped to keep it that way. They did unpleasant things to her stomach. Today would be no exception.

She stepped in, followed by Leviticus. He pushed a button and the doors swooshed closed behind them, her fate sealed. She reached back, blindly searching for the handrail to steady her footing.

A bell dinged somewhere on the silver panel. The door slid open with another whoosh, exposing polished cream-colored tiled floors and a brightly lit corridor. A man dressed in a janitorial uniform stepped on and nodded their way. His work shirt declared his name was Ralph.

Verity watched as he positioned his rake-thin body against the side of the elevator. Perhaps he didn't like riding in it any more than she did.

They rode up two floors together in total silence. With a will of its own, the shiny metal door swished open. At a distance, Verity noticed a crescent-shaped nurses' station. A cluster of nurses dressed in cheerful scrubs mingled close by. One hospital caregiver looked up and gazed at them. Verity had grown accustomed to *Englisch* curiosity.

Completely out of character, and something he hadn't done since their courting days, Leviticus grabbed her hand and pulled her out of the elevator. Surprised, she stumbled forward and would have lost her footing if he hadn't pulled her close. "Are you all right?"

"Ya." Her face warmed. The man named

Ralph slipped past and disappeared down a long hallway to their right.

Leviticus nodded, and together they moved forward, walking in unison.

If she remembered correctly, Albert's room was located two floors below. *So why did we get off on the fourth floor?*

Tethered to him by the warm grasp of his fingers, she hurried alongside him. "Wait!"

He paused abruptly, causing her to bump into his arm. He gazed down at her, one pale brow arched in curiosity. "You've changed your mind about seeing my *daed*?"

She had forgotten how tall he was, and handsome. She shook her head, ignoring the thrill tickling her stomach. *This foolishness must stop.* "*Nee*, of course I didn't change my mind." She glanced back at the elevator, toward the nurses. "Didn't we get off on the wrong floor?" She pulled her hand away from his and instantly regretted the loss of his touch.

After running his hand across his grizzled chin, he shoved his hands in his pockets.

"They moved *Daed* to this room early this morning. After fresh tests were run and his doctor examined him."

"Oh." She noticed how quiet the halls were, how silently the nurses interacted with each other. "Is this an ICU ward?"

"No. Not exactly. It's the hospice unit."

"Hospice?" Verity's chin wobbled. She was all too familiar with the medical term. Her *grossmudder* had lived out her last days hooked up to a morphine drip in a ward just like this one. The possibility of Albert's demise became very real to her in that moment. "I'm very sorry your father's worse."

"*Ya.*" His shoulders rounded, his eyes bloodshot from lack of sleep. He looked exhausted. "I should have come back to Pinecraft sooner."

"Some will say you came home too late, but at least you *did* come home." She wished she could say any number of things that would make him feel less guilty. But the fact remained that he had taken off, left his father to worry about the fate of the family grove. And there wasn't a doubt in her mind that Leviticus had enjoyed his time in the *Englischer* world.

"Like anything I do can make a difference now." He cupped her elbow as he directed her down the short corridor to a room at the end of the hall.

"You have to know you coming home made a big difference to Albert."

He shrugged, his glace quick. "I guess it did." He rubbed his hand down his arm. "Don't be too alarmed when you see him." His expression became grim. "*Daed* might look pretty bad." His steps slowed and stopped in front of a door. "His heart's tired. Maybe giving out. We have to prepare ourselves for what might happen."

His words entered her brain, but their meaning didn't register. Time slipped away. Young Leviticus stood before her, vulnerable and grief stricken. She allowed herself to linger in the past, remembering the good times, when all that mattered was the color of the dress she wore to church and if Leviticus would approve of how she looked in it.

"Unless something changes, he could die tonight." His chin dropped, but then he looked up, his tear-filled eyes holding her gaze. "It's important we act strong." He wiped his big palm across his cheek, removing a trail of tears. "I don't know if I can pull it off." He laughed ruefully. "I've never been much of an actor." Immense pain showed clearly on his face.

Her heart raced. She read the signs of grief, saw the bags under his eyes. He was hurting badly.

Verity blinked back tears of sympathy. Her chest ached. These were the most honest words she'd heard him utter since he'd been a young man and walked out of her life. She mustered up every ounce of courage she possessed, her head nodding in unspoken encouragement. "*Ya*, you can pull it off, Leviticus. You have to."

She struggled inwardly for the right words, and suddenly they came. "We draw strength from the Lord. *Gott* promises to see us through hard times like these." She forgot about her anger bubbling just under the surface since he'd come home, about her anger at him for leaving and breaking her heart. Her resentment didn't seem so important now. Albert might be dying.

With a mind of their own, the tips of her fingers brushed across his cheek, the stubble growing on his chin scraping against their pads. Old emotions tried to flare back to life in a fire that would consume her heart forever if she let it.

She pulled her fingers away and forced a half grin. "Let's go see your *daed*. He's waiting."

Leviticus thought he'd prepared himself for his father's appearance, but he hadn't and evidently neither had Verity. He heard her shocked gasp. His *daed*'s body seemed to have shriveled overnight, his coloring so pale it looked translucent against the hospital bed's white sheets. His heart breaking, he listened to the sounds his father made as he gasped for air through dry, cracked lips. Someone had pushed his father's long gray hair off his forehead, exposing the old man's rawboned features. How had he lost so much weight so quickly?

He clutched Verity's arm, as much to support himself as to steady her. She was seeing what he saw, and yet she stood strong and unwavering. But he knew her bravado was just an act. Somehow, she always thought she had to be the strong one, to set a standard far too high for her to maintain for long. He acknowledged his brother standing at the foot of the bed, and then Otto seated next to him with a nod. "Sit here." He led Verity to the chair just vacated by Otto at the side of his father's bed.

Dressed smartly in pressed dark trousers, black suspenders and a white shirt good enough to be his Sunday best, Otto had aged during the years Leviticus had been away. But the short, stout man appeared sturdy and unyielding as he moved closer to Albert's side.

As best he could remember, Otto's finest official bishop's garb was reserved for special occasions, like weddings and social events of the highest caliber. If his father had awakened, he would have no doubt been honored by the man's display of respect and loyalty. Almost the same age, the men had been friends since *bus*. He knew Otto loved Albert, yet their competitive checker games at the park had often been loud and amusing. Still in shock over his father's declined health, Leviticus stumbled down to the foot of the bed.

Otto moved restlessly about the room, standing for a moment with Leviticus, only to relinquish the spot to Solomon and wander to a spare chair by the door. As the slightly bent man glanced around and observed their faces, he touched his beard, drawing his short, stubby fingers down the length of the bristled hair. He showed his edginess by stretching out the collar of his shirt with one finger, something Leviticus remembered seeing him do a thousand times while he would preach.

Albert suddenly opened his eyes and made a sound, surprising them all. He didn't move his head but sought to stare at Leviticus's face with eyes the color of a summer sky. Eyes so like his own. Deep emotions, feelings he thought he'd long forgotten, stirred, causing him to gasp for breath. This was the father he knew and loved as a child. Albert looked near death, but in his mind, his *daed* was still the strong, single-minded father he remembered all too well. It was as if he could read the old man's thoughts. Soh, *have you wed yet?*

He pulled his gaze away from his father's and looked toward Verity. She had sidled up to him by the bed, hovering, her face twisted in concern. There was no doubt in his mind. She loved his father as much as her own. In that moment, he knew they would marry today and bring peace to the old man's mind before he passed. She would obey Otto's wishes. She was Amish raised, just like Albert. Their motto was God's will be done.

Her chin lifted, her eyes locking with his for a moment. Silent words were exchanged between them. There *would* be a wedding today, like it or not. The time to fight Otto had passed. They would become man and wife, here and now, in this hospital room. Verity nodded his way, silently like-minded. Her shoulders dropped, all resistance gone.

Reading their signs of resignation, Otto stepped forward, his Bible in hand. "For the love of Albert, I'm setting aside the rules of membership before marriage."

As minutes passed, Leviticus realized most of the formality of traditional Amish weddings was being set aside also. Leviticus looked into the eyes of his father's best friend. There would be a fuss raised among the congregation, but Otto stood steady on his feet, prepared to set aside whatever was needed for his lifelong friend.

Amish marriages were till death do us

part. This was a huge sacrifice from Verity. Come Sunday, he'd join the New Order Amish church and finally be in good standing with the community. But what would his standing with Verity be after today?

Traditional questions of loyalty to the church and each other would be left unasked and unanswered for today. There were to be no cheerful songs sung, laced with *Gott*'s promise to the faithful. It didn't matter that he and Verity had no friends seated at their side, no wedding meal waiting for them at home. There'd be no family visits in other states, no days of visiting friends. *Will Verity feel cheated?* Naturally, she would.

Otto motioned Solomon over, cleared his voice and bowed his head. All in the room followed suit. Leviticus's fingers fumbled as he removed his baseball cap and tossed it on the floor. Why hadn't he cut his hair sooner, taken to wearing Amish garb before now? Verity would have wanted that for today.

Am I ready to be Amish? He reached out and took her cold hand in his. Her body quaked next to him. Marriage was forever. They both knew it. She was as terrified as he was. Maybe more.

Otto lifted his chin and spoke. "Before *Gott*, we are here to join this man and this woman in the bonds of holy matrimony."

Leviticus didn't know where to look. He fixed his eyes across from his father's bed, on a simple watercolor of rolling hills and meadows, where cows grazed in the bright sunshine. He forced his mind to go blank. Still, memories of his *mamm*'s last words to his *daed* screamed inside his head. *I love you, my husband. I always will.* Love was meant to be eternal. What they were doing was wrong. Marriage was sacred to Verity, something most woman went into after much consideration and prayer. Surely, she required a measure of love from the man standing next to her.

Did he love Verity? The *Englischer* life had taught him to respect women, allow them to have a mind of their own, do what they thought best for themselves. He felt affection—but love her the way a man should love his woman? What did he know about that kind of love?

Albert and her family shouldn't be selling Verity off to him like a plot of land to be kept in the family. Especially to someone who had more mental issues than she knew about. *She has a right to know whom she's getting.* Would she have considered him worthy if she understood the depth of sins he'd committed? Not in a million years. She deserved a whole man, someone who could love her the way her first husband had loved her. She'd compare him to Mark. Who could blame her?

Solomon moved in closer, stood next to Verity as if to protect her from Leviticus. She might well need Solomon's protection. He thought of his remaining depression, his temper when riled, thanks to the remains of PTSD.

"Those *Gott* has joined together, let no man put asunder," Otto's words ended. They were man and wife, *Gott* help her.

The room echoed with silence. He looked down, saw Verity's true feelings written on her face. She was ashen, limp, her lips drooping at the corners. Her eyes swam with tears. She glanced up at him through pale lashes, her glassy-eyed stare unsettling him. *She's shut down.* He'd seen men shut down on the battlefield. Hadn't he done the same to keep what little sanity he had a year ago? He held tight to her fingers, fearing she'd pull away and reject him at the last moment.

Albert made a noise in his throat. Otto motioned her over. Verity hurried closer to his father's bed. Leviticus joined her, contemplating their situation. He looked at his father's face. His eyes were closed, but a peaceful smile tugged at the corners of his mouth. A knot in Leviticus's stomach grew. His father was still alive but could have easily slipped away as Otto spoke words of love and trust over them, joining them as one.

Otto stepped behind them. "Leave him for now. He needs rest."

Verity jerked her hand away and pressed

it to her pale lips. She gasped for air and then rushed from the room, the skirt of her plain blue dress flying behind her. He made a move to follow, but Solomon's hand caught him roughly by the arm. "Let her go, *bruder*. She needs to be alone."

He jerked his arm away. "*Nee!* She needs me. She's my *fraa* now."

"*Ya*, she may be your *fraa*, but only because her love for *Daed* forced her into this union. She has no need of you. She needs time to gather her thoughts." Solomon's eyes burned with anger, his mouth an unforgiving line of contempt.

Leviticus hurried out the door and down the hall, all the way to the empty elevators. Verity was nowhere in sight. He looked back toward the hallway, beyond his father's room. Had she taken the stairs at the end of the short hall?

He stood on the edge of insanity, alone and without wisdom. He didn't know how to feel, what to think. He shook inwardly. His shoulders carried a heavy burden of guilt as he made his way back into his father's room. This marriage arrangement had provided a mother for his tiny daughter, but what of Verity? What had she gained by it? An empty shell of a man.

Chapter Twelve

The toe of Verity's flip-flop caught on the top stair, sending her stumbling across the wooden porch of the old farmhouse. The sun had finally come out, making her walk from the hospital a long hot one. Sweat trickled down her neck, trailed down her spine.

Catching a ride on the back of Les Yoder's cart at the edge of Sarasota had been a true blessing. Her mind swirled from the events of the day. She'd remained silent when Les dropped her off at the grove gate and waved goodbye as he drove off. She told him about Albert's worsening condition, but not that she'd married his *soh*. The community would find out soon enough, and what would they think?

Leviticus and I married. How can it be?

Not willing to let her new husband fill her thoughts, she pictured Albert instead. His shallow, labored breathing still haunted her.

Will he live? Please, Gott. *Let him live.*

She'd learned death was a part of life, something she had to accept as the Lord's will, but losing the sweet old man was unthinkable. She had her strong faith to fall back on, but what about Leviticus? Was he truly a believer now or putting on an act just to please his father? Try as she would, she couldn't understand why *Gott* would want to snatch Albert away, especially now that Leviticus was home.

She'd never been close to her own father. Oh, he was kind to her and loving on occasion, but he was a hardworking man, someone who gave more of himself to his profession as a cabinetmaker than to his family. She'd been raised predominately by her *mamm*. As a child, she longed for a father who shared his wisdom and kind heart with her. She found those qualities in Albert when she came to work for him.

Now I'm tethered to Leviticus, a man who doesn't love me.

She entered the great room and called out to Clara. Silence greeted her. She breathed a sigh of relief. She needed a moment to collect her thoughts and calm down before she told Clara that she and Leviticus had married.

She moved through the familiar rooms of the house, toward her bedroom, and found a note attached to Albert's favorite chair with a large safety pin. She unfolded the slip of paper and recognized her mother's neat script. *I've got the girls with me and will return later in the day. Clara's gone to the hospital to be with Solomon.*

Perhaps she should have stayed with Leviticus. He was her husband after all. But the day had proven to be too much for her. Running away showed the weak side of her she wasn't proud of. Albert would have expected more of her now that she was his *soh*'s *fraa*.

Tears blurred her vision. She began to refold the paper and then noticed a scribble in purple marker just under her mother's message. A smiley face and Faith's name had been carefully drawn and printed at the bottom of the page. She half smiled. Her sweet girl might have her father's above-average intelligence, but she had Verity's terrible handwriting. She tucked the paper in her apron pocket and continued down the hall, past Albert's room, the back of her hand wiping a fresh tear from her cheek.

She shuffled through her bedroom door on rubbery legs. Inside, everything was neat and tidy as usual. Her bedroom window was open a crack, the lightweight curtains at her window dancing in the wind. It had been in the low sixties for days thanks to the hurricane, but now it had rained again, and the Florida humidity was back with a vengeance.

Moments later, a sound behind her made

her turn and look. Leviticus stood just inside the dimly lit hall. “When did you come home?”

“Just now. You shouldn’t leave the main door unlocked when you’re alone.”

Amish people seldom locked doors, but he was right. “*Ya*, times are changing. I’ll have to form new habits now that Albert’s not in the house.” She dropped her voice, her words falling off into a deep dark well of misery. She was sure he wasn’t ready to discuss their impromptu marriage or his father’s worsening health any more than she was. She looked up, saw pain etched deep on his face.

He stood stoop-shouldered, as if he were an old man.

“Solomon and Clara are with you?” she asked. Inch by inch, she edged toward her bedroom door. Her bare toes curled under as she paused just outside the door.

“No. I left them comforting each other. Clara mentioned they’d soon be going back to their own place—in a week, perhaps more. The workers are almost finished with the repairs to their house. There was nothing I could say or do to help *Daed*." Leviticus looked hard at her, his eyes searching. "I had to come home, see if you were okay."

"Of course I am."

Their words echoed through the quiet house and died.

He said what she'd been thinking. "The place feels empty without him, doesn't it? Like *Daed* is the heart of this home and without him here there is no home." He wiped a tear from his cheek with the back of his hand, but it was replaced by a fresh one.

She took a step toward him and then another, compassion and her own pain drawing them together in misery. She grabbed his limp hand. It was cold and trembling. He'd left the grove when his *mamm* died. Would he leave the grove again if Albert passed?

Somehow, she found herself wrapped in his arms, his tears dampening her shoulder as he wept like a child. They swayed together as one, grief and concern for Albert tearing away all past angers in that moment in time.

Her ear pressed against his chest. She heard his heart beat as he took in quick, unsteady breaths. Moments passed. The old clock in the great room chimed. He hadn't moved in minutes, but his arms were lax now, almost limp at his sides. She took in a deep breath, prepared to move.

"I'm sorry," he murmured, stepping away. "I don't know what came over me. I didn't mean to embarrass you." He rubbed at the gristle on his chin, his hand sliding down to grasp the back of his neck.

"Don't be silly. You didn't embarrass me," she insisted, even though she felt heat warming her face. "You needed comfort. We both did. I love Albert, too, you know." She cleared the roughness from her voice. "Let me get changed and I'll fix a quick meal."

He looked down the hall, toward his bedroom. "I'm not up to eating right now. I have a headache."

"I'll get you something to drink instead." She took another step back.

"Yeah, sure. That would be great." He ran his hand through his long, tangled hair, went to move down the hall and then turned back around. "I'll wait for you in the kitchen. Okay?"

Verity backed up against her door, her hand grasping the knob. "*Ya*, just give me a moment."

He nodded and then ambled off, his head down.

She hurried into her room, shut the door firmly behind her and slipped out of the old blue dress that had become her wedding dress. With little interest in what she wore, she grabbed one of her everyday dresses and left her apron and prayer *kapp* on the bed. Still barefoot, she hurried into the hallway. Albert would want her to see to his son's needs now that she was his wife.

The reality of her situation hit like a ton of

bricks. She paused. The wedding… Everything had happened so fast. She hadn't had time to absorb any of it or come to terms with the new position she held in this household. A jumble of thoughts rushed in, more concerning than before. She turned back toward the opened bedroom door. Would he expect to share that bed with her tonight?

She shoved her shoulders back and marched away from the bedroom door. "*Ya*, well. He can think again," she whispered to the silent hall. "I'm not prepared for any such matters of the heart."

The kitchen still smelled faintly of bacon. Leviticus grabbed the pot of old coffee from that morning and placed it back on the gas burner to reheat. Blue flames licked around the bottom of the old metal pot. The brew would be bitter, but he didn't care. Military life had taught him to like his coffee strong.

As he moved around the room, he looked out the kitchen window. The wind was kicking up again, wildly blowing a set of white sheets someone had hung on the line earlier. He took down a thick mug from the cupboard, poured the dark steaming liquid in and then jerked out a wooden chair. The mug thumped loudly as he placed it in front of him. His hands were trembling again, his PTSD rearing its ugly head. He tried to relax, forced his breath to be deep and regulated.

But his mind would not stop racing, no matter how hard he tried to master the art of bringing every thought into captivity as the Bible suggested.

If only I had a breathing technique for that.

A headache at the base of his skull thumped hard, reminding him to take one of his little blue pills or he'd be sorry later. The headaches had started in Afghanistan, long before he'd been shot and almost killed.

Memories of the war flooded in. Running for cover during a barrage of gunfire, he'd taken a fall and hit his head on a rock. He'd seen stars but hadn't gotten the bleeding goose egg seen to. There was no time. The doctors were busy saving brave men's lives.

He stared down into the coffee and then slowly sipped, welcoming the unpleasant, bitter taste as something infinitely familiar. He'd experienced a lot of losses the last few years. The loss of his army buddies who never made it home, the loss of his way of life as part of a troop. He was glad when they released him from the army on a medical discharge. No more wars. No more moving. He could give Naomi the stable life she deserved as an Amish child with a mother by her side. But still, the ground didn't seem solid under his feet. He was attempting to live his old Amish way of life again, embrace old ways of thinking, and some days failing miserably.

He looked down at his jeans, tugged at the sleeve of his knit T-shirt. It was past time. All this garb would have to go. It was the behavioral changes that would challenge him most. He was a father now, *and* husband, too. His shoulders lifted and fell.

Would *Gott* show him the way to complete redemption? Could he do right by Verity, their daughters? He pushed the coffee cup away, his stomach too acidic from nerves.

He ought to be able to relax about Naomi's future now, but what about Verity's and Faith's futures with him as head of the house? His daughter would have a loving mother, a big family who loved her. They'd meet her needs better than he could alone. He and Naomi profited from the marriage, but Verity and Faith had come out with the short end of the stick.

The kitchen door swung open with a squeak. Verity entered the room wearing a plain dark blue dress without an apron. She approached gingerly and set a stack of clothes on the table next to him.

"These were Solomon's things. Clara thought she'd help out and selected them for you a few days ago." She let her hand linger on the roughly sewn trousers on top of the pile. "The pants may be a bit short. Solomon's not as tall as you."

"Danki." Leviticus noticed a pair of suspenders tucked under the edge of the pants. They looked new, like Verity had bought them specially for him.

"Here, let me make you a fresh mug of coffee." She whisked his cup away and busied herself cleaning the coffeepot and filling it with fresh water and grinds. "You shouldn't have heated that coffee."

"I like it strong."

Verity made a sound with her tongue, like a mother duck clucking her disapproval at her foolish *kind*. "There's no need for you to drink stale coffee. You have a *fraa* now, someone to make sure you eat well and dress properly."

He set aside the suspenders and fingered the woven cotton shirt on the bottom of the pile of clothing. It was made of rough woven cotton, snaps instead of buttons closing the front. He favored knit T-shirts in warm weather. "Dress properly, as in Amish trousers and a plain shirt?" He smiled at her, trying to keep their conversation light. "You know I hate wearing suspenders."

She twisted around, her hands still busy adding soap shavings to the running dish-water. "But you are an Amish *mann* now. Plain. Love it or hate it, these are the clothes you'll need to wear to please your *daed* and the community. Did you think you could keep dressing like an *Englischer*? You're married, soon to be a member of this community. Changes have to be made."

"I know." His tone held more rancor than he'd intended. "I'd planned on buying suitable clothes the next time I went into town. I just never found the time."

Verity turned back, abandoning the cup she'd been washing. Her eyes narrowed. "Remember, clothes don't make the *mann*. You'll have to change your way of thinking, too, to become a true *mann* of faith."

He heard her sniff, saw her shoulders square as she turned back to the dishes. Was she fighting tears again? A tenderness came over him. Verity was a good woman. She should be sitting quietly, calming her frazzled nerves, not taking care of his needs. She'd been through a lot. Spirited or not, she had a gentle Amish heart. His guilt piled high, causing his head to pound harder.

"Take some ibuprofen. I can see your head is hurting again by the way you're squinting." She dried her hands and hung up the dishcloth. "There's a bottle of tablets on the table, next to the napkins." She pointed just past his hand.

"Thanks, but I've got something."

Why didn't she sit?

"I appreciate all you've done for me, for Naomi and for my *vadder*. You know that, right?"

She lifted the coffeepot, poured a steaming cup and handed it to him. "Today, I didn't do any of it for you, Leviticus. I did it for Albert. He's been good to me and never asked for anything back but kindness. Marrying you was the least I could do for him."

Leviticus shook his head in regret. She was trapped in a loveless marriage thanks to his return. "I appreciate your sacrifice, Verity. I do. I promise I'll try to be a good husband and love Faith as if she were my own child."

Verity's chin quivered as she spoke. "I'll hold you to that promise. My *dochder* is not going to suffer because I made a pledge to an *Englischer* who's playing at being Amish for the sake of his father."

Her words stung, but he saw them as true. The main reason he had come home was to attempt a reunion with his father and brother, but his new awareness of God's love had spurred him on, too. Marrying Verity and being a father to Faith had never been part of his plans. But he'd keep his promise to her or die trying. He owed her that much.

Verity pulled out a kitchen chair and joined him at the table. She slumped back, as tired as he suspected.

"We have more to talk about." Her gaze didn't meet his. "From the beginning, I need to make something clear."

Her tone was much too serious for his

liking. "Okay." He braced himself for her words. His hand moved, pushing away the cup of coffee untouched.

"Our union may be blessed by *Gott* and the church." She paused, took a deep breath and then continued on, "But I won't be sleeping in your bed. We are no love match. Not anymore." She smoothed out an imaginary wrinkle in the tablecloth in front of her, her gaze downward.

He understood her reluctance for intimacy only too well. "I didn't expect anything more from you, Verity. All I need is kindness for my daughter. I'm satisfied with our arrangement and see no need for change now, or in the future."

Her words didn't hurt him. He'd built too many walls around his heart to be wounded.

Chapter Thirteen

The next morning, the first signs of an early fall blew in on a brisk, cold wind from the far north. Verity woke from a fitful sleep, disoriented at first, but the aroma of coffee brewing had her slipping out of bed before the rooster crowed. She threw on her robe, changed Naomi's soaked diaper and then made her way to the kitchen for some much-needed caffeine and a bottle for Naomi.

Leviticus didn't look any better than she felt as he greeted her with an unsure smile. "*Guder mariye.* I see from the bags under your eyes, you slept about as well as I did."

Self-conscious, she silently nodded. She

hadn't bothered to repair her braid. Her hand went straight to her hair, but she noticed his blond hair was as wild and uncombed as her own must be.

She smiled and nodded her thank-you when he set a hot cup of coffee on the table for her. Doing battle with a squirming Naomi, she slipped the soon-to-be one-year-old into the high chair and poured out a handful of dry oat cereal for her to eat while her bottle heated.

Faith hurried into the kitchen without house shoes on her feet and hugged her *mamm* from behind, rubbing sleep from her eyes as she made her way to a chair.

"Did you sleep well, *liebling*?"

"*Ya*, but Naomi woke me just now with her crying." Eyes as dark as Verity's coffee shot her new *schweschder* an accusing glance.

Verity coughed against her shoulder, her allergies kicking up from the brisk winds blowing outside. She downed a gulp of coffee as she made her way to the refrigerator for milk. "She's little, not quite a year old. You cried just like her when you were a *boppli*."

Today was Sunday, their first real day of married life and the grove's day to host members of the church for lunch. Word would spread, and she and Leviticus would be greeted as a married couple. Her nerves kicked up her stomach, but she fought down the urge to fall into dread.

It would be a cold breakfast for everyone, but first, Faith needed telling about the wedding before someone else informed her during the church service.

Leviticus worked on his own cup of steaming brew across from Faith while Verity downed the last of her coffee and gathered her courage to speak to her sleepy daughter.

"I have news I'm certain-sure you're going to like, Faith."

"Ya?" Faith said with about as much enthusiasm as Verity felt.

"Leviticus and I were married yesterday."

Leviticus looked up, seeking her gaze, his expression priceless. He hadn't been prepared for Faith's bellow of joy and neither had Verity. No doubt, Faith's explosion had woken Pinecraft and the outer edges of Sarasota proper.

Scared by Faith's ruckus, Naomi let loose a squall of her own. Verity lifted the child from the high chair, comforted her and watched as Leviticus squirmed as Faith rained kisses on his face and gave him hug after hug.

"I knew you two were in love. I could see it in your eyes," Faith said with a giggle.

Cool and controlled, Leviticus agreed. "*Ya*, it was love at first sight, ain't so, Verity? You knew best," he said to the child, with a forced smile he shared with Verity.

Calmed now, Naomi was set on a pallet near the table for her father to see to as Verity took down bowls and gathered her wits about her. All this talk of love unnerved her.

A secret glance back her husband's way had her breath catching in her throat. Glowing with confidence, Naomi grabbed hold of her *daed*'s pant leg and pulled herself up like she'd been doing it for weeks. Her first tentative steps were cautious but without assistance. A smile lifted Leviticus's mouth and brightened his eyes. Keeping guard, Leviticus's hands were there to catch Naomi when her tiny legs grew tired and she toppled over.

Leviticus cheered, but she held back a little of herself for fear she'd grow too fond of this normal setting of peaceful family life. *Lord, keep me ever faithful to Your will.*

Leviticus made a face, shaving under his nose and then critically examining the beginning of his pale beard. *Pathetic!* It would take some time for it to grow and even more time getting used to the look of it, but for now the itching on his chin was worse than the change in appearance. He dressed carefully, putting on one of the new homemade trousers and long-sleeved shirts he'd bought from Mose's wife, Sarah, the night before.

Just as he'd rinsed his face and toweled it dry, his phone went off. *Daed?* He lifted the small thin device and placed it next to his ear. “Hello.”

“Good morning, Mr. Hilty. This is June Hillsborough, your dad’s morning nurse. Do you have a moment to talk?”

Nerves curled in Leviticus’s stomach. Each time the phone rang, and it was the hospital, he wondered if this was the call. Had his *daed* gotten worse? Perhaps even died?

“*Ya*, sure.” The beat of his heart increased in his ears to a deafening roar.

“I’m sorry to be calling so early. I know you have young children. I didn’t want to wake them, but I thought you’d be glad to know we’re beginning to see some marked improvement in your father’s lab work. He seems to be responding well to his new heart medication, and his diet is making a real difference in his kidney function. His kidney and liver functions are much improved this morning. Also, his blood oxygen levels are up. All good signs he’s beginning to progress.” The nurse cleared her throat. “Naturally we'll be taking more blood through the day and continuing to monitor his oxygen levels to make sure he remains stable, but all and all we're seeing good reports and plan to move him to a step-down room soon."

Leviticus took in a calming breath and pushed it back out again. "*Danki* for calling me. Have you spoken to Solomon, my *bruder*, this morning?"

"Yes, I did just a moment ago. Like you, he seemed relieved. Well, I'd best get back to my patients. You have yourself a great day."

"You, too," Leviticus said, his relief laced in his voice. Punching the red icon on his phone and hanging up, Leviticus leaned against the dresser he'd used as a *kind* and groaned in relief, his head down, eyes closed. A tear slipped from his eye, and then another. He needed *gut* news. Needed something concrete like a good report to hang on to. But would his father's recovery have Verity regretting their marriage vows already?

Five minutes later, after a moment of

calming prayer, he strolled into the kitchen and couldn't help but laugh out loud as he watched Verity try to catch Naomi, who was quickly crawling around on the kitchen floor, doing her best to avoid being picked up. Determination was written all over her chubby face, and his *dochder*'s dark curls and eyes shone bright in the early-morning sun. She scurried along toward him in an awkward crab-like crawl, her tiny body clad in the violet-colored dress he had watched Verity complete sewing the night before.

"If you'll just catch her and hold her, I'll finish dressing her," Verity said, doing her best to place the *kind*'s *kapp* on Naomi's head.

Holding the squirming *boppli* while Verity slipped on the child's tiny apron, he grinned Verity's way as she fought a mighty battle to hold Naomi's twisting head as she adjusted her prayer *kapp*. He was surprised to see Verity putting small dabs of sticky molasses on each side of the child's head before the final adjustment was made.

Verity grinned at him. "What? You thought *kapps* stayed on *bopplis* without a little help? She doesn't have enough hair for pins."

"A *mamm* always knows best," he muttered and then nodded his approval as Faith came prancing in, fully dressed, proclaiming she'd gotten herself ready. Her apron was tied in a messy knot at the back, but Verity was obviously proud of her daughter's accomplishments and let it be. "You did a *gut* job, Faith. Ain't so, Leviticus?"

He nodded like a proud *daed* would, amazed at how well their first morning as a family was going. He'd expected… Well, he didn't know what he'd expected, but not this feeling of delight.

"I'm the big *schweschder* now. I don't need help dressing anymore."

He sidled up to Verity as she poured round dry cereal in a bag for Naomi. "There was a call from the hospital."

Verity froze in motion, her eyes searching his, brows knitting. "Is Albert all right?"

"It's *gut* news, *fraa.* Calm yourself. His

bloodwork is showing improvement and the nurse was decidedly more positive this call." Leviticus watched the stress ease from Verity's face and smiled. "*Gott*'s will for Albert's life, ain't so?"

"*Ya*, *Gott*'s will." A smile blossomed on her face.

A few moments later, warm capes and *kapps* were put on and then Leviticus shut the back door behind them. He led the way down the stairs with Naomi squirming in his arms, finally feeling like an Amish family *mann*.

"Are you nervous?" Verity asked, walking close to his side along the gravel road.

"About?" he asked, and then realized what she meant. He was joining the church today. His stomach flopped, but he smiled anyway. "*Nee*, not nervous. More like relieved. I should have done this a long time ago." What he was doing this morning felt right to him. Just like holding Faith's hand when Verity took over the care of Naomi as they strolled along.

She hadn't had time to digest the fact that his *daed* was improving. Soon enough he'd see if their marriage of convenience would work out or not. The thought of Verity tied to him all her life and regretting it worked on his nerves, but he knew how to pray nowadays. Prayer made a difference. Probably it always had, and he'd been too stupid to realize it.

Lines of men were already forming at the door of the church as they approached. He left Verity and the children with the ladies gathered on the grass and strolled up behind several married men in line.

Otto greeted him with a firm handshake, as he did all the men and women standing around, but while he held on to Leviticus's hand he asked, "Is all well? A lot of changes have taken place in a short period of time for you, ain't so?"

Leviticus nodded.

"Albert is better?"

"*Ya*, much better than we'd hoped. The nurse called while I was dressing. *Daed*'s improved. She said they would be moving him to a step-down room sometime today, but still watching his vitals closely."

"*Gut*, this is progress." Otto smiled his approval. "And Verity? She is well?"

"She and the children are fine."

With a nod, Otto slipped to the next man in line and greeted him, leaving Leviticus with his thoughts. Happiness filled him. His father was improving, and Verity showed her relief at the news by being easygoing all morning. If someone had been watching them interact, they would have thought them a normal Amish family. But he had noticed Verity watching him with wary eyes a moment before, as if she expected him to morph back into the man he'd been when he'd first come home.

Keep me learning and growing, Gott. *Bless my father with* gut *health. Return him to us.*

Her mind dwelling on Albert's improvement, Verity pushed away the jumble of nerves that had been eating at her. She peered out the kitchen door, and like a longtime married woman, looked around for her husband's help. There were tables to be moved and benches to be put in their place. She'd been busy after they'd walked home from church and lost track of him in the growing crowd of hungry people. *Where had he disappeared to?*

She shut the door and skirted around several volunteers who'd come to help arrange food platters and containers of peanut butter brought for the after-service meal. "Excuse me." Her mind was full of things still needing to be done. There were cold drinks to be made, a vegetable platter to be put together. But deep inside she was smiling like a silly *bensel*, content the *kinner* were happy and all was well. Albert was better, and Leviticus had finally become a member of the church.

A dark thought crept in, overshadowing her joy. What about the trap of marriage she'd stepped into? Would happiness remain? Content or not, she'd have to accept her lot in life until the day she died. *Please, Lord, Your will for my life and for Leviticus.*

It had been a while since she'd been able to check on Naomi. She hurried over to the corner and found the *boppli* still fast asleep in her mesh playpen cluttered with toys and a snuggle blanket.

Back at the kitchen sink a moment later, Verity washed dishes as her mind slipped away to that morning. Faith had been so thrilled to learn Leviticus was her *daed*. She smiled at the memory as she looked out the window and noticed Leviticus walking up the hill with one of the church pastors, deep in conversation.

A warm flush settled over her. Maybe it wasn't contentment she was feeling. How could it be? She was married to a man she didn't love. Didn't really know. She fought to fight down the stress eating at her. Her mother had always told her to find something to be grateful for and she settled on, *I'm grateful for my life as a* mamm.

"Hand me a stack of those paper plates?" Sarah Fischer asked, bringing Verity back to the present. A moment later, her hands busy washing cutting boards and utensils, she returned to her musing. As they'd walked home from church, Leviticus had smiled so attentively at Faith as the *kinner* chattered on, telling him all about the swings she'd swung on the day before and how, now that they were a *familye*, they could go to the park and have a swinging contest of their own.

Leviticus enjoyed Faith's run-on sentences and loud laughter. She was used to her daughter's exuberance. The child had been a chatterbox since she'd started uttering single syllable words, but for Leviticus to be so kind and patient with Faith gave her hope for their future.

Again, she was pulled out of her reverie by Sarah, who was busy working circles around her. "Your potato salad looks good. Mose is sure to eat more than his share of yours."

They laughed together, and Verity sighed.

No one seemed to notice her up-and-down moods. Maybe they expected her to be happier than usual. She was a new *fraa.* It was only natural for her to be happy. She'd have to work harder at keeping her dark thoughts at bay and smile more.

"Congratulations on your marriage."

Verity placed a delicious-looking pineapple upside-down cake on the dessert table. *"Danki."* She smiled at Sarah, who was just beginning to show with yet another blessing from *Gott*. She wanted to confide in Sarah about the truth of her new marriage but ignored the urge. No need to spoil Sarah's good mood that washed her in a warm glow.

Verity accepted her friend's congratulations as if she were the happiest woman in Pinecraft. Truth be told, she was confused by her moments of joy while living a lie. Leviticus didn't love her, but she was trying to make do for Albert's sake. Perhaps Leviticus was going through the same states of confusion.

Time slipped past. The men started filing in, one by one. The faithful of Pinecraft seemed to be accepting her union with Leviticus as nothing more than a marriage brought on by renewed love.

But gossip was a staple in a town full of women in *kapps*. She'd heard snippets of conversation regarding Leviticus's sudden church membership, whispers about their quickie marriage while the women filed out of the church earlier. Most of the faithful, the important ones, seemed willing enough to accept Leviticus was home for good, and that was all that mattered. Albert was healing, and the girls had a *familye*, not just single parents. Their joy counted for something.

She wiped down the edge of the sink for the hundredth time as men continued to come inside in waves, eat and then slip back out to the yard, where they talked about needed repairs in the community. As she waited to eat with the other ladies, her mind roamed over the unusual circumstances of the last few days. Leviticus seemed to be trying hard to obey *Ordnung* rules, be the man his father wanted him to be since he had taken another turn for the better.

She was genuinely glad Leviticus had been allowed to re-embrace his Amish destiny, but what about Solomon's resentment toward Leviticus? And surely there were memories Leviticus brought home with him from the *Englisch* world he'd have to forget. Did he miss the *Englischer* way of doing things? Was he going to be content as an Amish man for the rest of his life?

Thankfully, the gentle part of him she'd grown to love as a girl was still there just under the surface. She'd seen glimpses of it and longed for a complete return of the old Leviticus.

Just as she'd collected the last of the men's dishes and added fresh bowls of food for the ladies, he sauntered in mud-streaked and sweaty, like the rest of the men who'd gone with him out into the grove to look at the damage.

She'd smiled at him as he stepped past,

watched his face as he took the plate of food she'd made him and grinned back when he flashed his dimple at her. Had the smile been forced? He seemed tense, like something was bothering him. Was it the condition of the grove?

While she served food to several ladies already seated, he lurked in the corner of the kitchen and then disappeared like a puff of smoke when she looked back. She dropped her gaze and silently prayed, *Help me to trust the future. Give Leviticus what he needs to be a Plain man.*

Ten minutes later, a silent prayer said by Theda Fischer, Otto's wife, ended the ladies' meal. Her head still bowed, she glanced over and witnessed Leviticus walking in through the back door. He looked across the kitchen, found her gaze and held it. She motioned for him to take the chair next to her.

Leviticus shook his head, grabbed a half sandwich off a plate stacked high, took a bite and threw it in the trash as he turned away from her.

"Ach," she muttered to herself. Often, she had to encourage him to eat. This morning, after hearing Leviticus's report about what the doctors had said about Albert's improvement, she'd gained hope that Albert's hard battle for life had been won. And Leviticus had seemed to believe it, as well. He'd relaxed. They'd had a good time walking to church, Faith on his shoulders and Naomi asleep in her arms. To her, they'd been the typical Amish family, but what had Leviticus thought? And there'd been no additional news about his father this afternoon, no reason to affirm her and Leviticus's continued hope.

She continued to study Leviticus when he wasn't aware, saw a haunted look on his face. At times, she noticed he clung to Naomi like a lifeline, as if his tiny daughter's love could save him from his own inner misery.

The kitchen still humming with the last of

the women finishing their meals, Leviticus appeared, speaking to Mose, who hovered near his wife with a toddler in his arms. Leviticus again excused himself and shouldered his way out the back door once more. Was he going out to talk to the other men milling around, slapping each other on the back and laughing at things only men could understand? Or was he going to his mother's grave, or out to the garage to tinker with his old truck?

In this restless mood he seemed to be in, she didn't know. She prayed once more for Albert's healing and for the man who was now her husband. Encouraging herself, she went through her litany of reminders. *He's changed since he's returned. Obeys community rules. Acts more mature.*

But as she washed plastic forks and spoons, she wondered, would Leviticus ever grow to love her? Only God knew the answer to that question. She knew her angry feelings toward him were still hanging between them. She cared about the man's concerns for his father, but it was pity she felt for him, wasn't it? That and nothing more?

Right? It had to be.

Chapter Fourteen

The last of the men headed out the back door with their wives in tow, leaving a capable handful of women to clean up the last of the mess in the kitchen. Verity plunged platters into the big kitchen sink filled with hot sudsy water, silent, her thoughts roaming.

Leviticus's sudden mood swings unnerved Verity when they came, but he'd never been mean-spirited to her or the girls. While he was silent and withdrawn, he seemed jumpier and more depressed than angry. But wasn't that to be expected? His father was ill. He felt guilty he'd stayed away so long. Albert might make it, but the hospital staff still offered no promises. She clung to each positive report from the doctors as a sign from *Gott*. He had heard her prayers. Albert would live.

Deep in thought as she scrubbed another big dish, curiosity got the better of her. What had happened to Leviticus during his life in the *Englisch* world?

She turned her head, watching again through the kitchen window as Leviticus slowly made his way down the hill toward the shed. Faith and Naomi seemed to be the only ones who could reach him whenever he was silent like this, so deep in thought.

On impulse, she turned Faith over to her younger sister's care and straddled Naomi on her hip as she followed where her new husband had gone, out the door and down the grassy slope. But she hesitated just feet away from the porch steps as Otto began to sing the words to Albert's favorite hymn. She stayed, singing the words to "In the Garden," one of the songs she'd often sung with Albert, their voices blending well in harmony.

Otto's eyes lifted, speaking to the people

of the community lingering around the back steps. "*Gott* is all knowing. In His wisdom, He may see fit to take Albert home or leave him here fit and back to health. Who here can question His motives?"

The old bishop fingered his gray beard, his head lowering in respect for the man he called his friend. "We rejoice in the majesty of the Lord and carry on as we always do, as any loved one prepares to go home." A tear glistened in the old bishop's eye and was quickly blinked away, but to Verity they revealed his true level of pain. "Now, let's be on our way to our homes and return tomorrow to work this grove back into shape. It's been a long day of worship and food. Clara and Verity both look ready to drop with fatigue."

Her knitting bag in hand, Theda sidled up to Verity. She nodded toward Naomi, who squirmed in Verity's arms. "That *boppli* is growing so fast. It won't be long before she's starting school, like Faith. You wait and see.

Time has a way of flying past. Enjoy her young years while you can."

Naomi smiled a toothless grin and reached out her arms to Theda. Verity handed her over.

"This one is an added blessing to your family. She already has joy in her eyes. You are a blessed woman, Verity. Not everyone gets a second chance with first love."

Verity smiled at the older woman. Leviticus had come home nothing like the boy she'd known, but she didn't have to tell Theda that. He'd come home an *Englischer* in actions and dress, but day by day she was seeing subtle changes in him, and all for the better. Would the changes last? He would never be the Amish *mann* she'd fallen hard for as a teen, but he was a good man now. "Naomi is my *dochder*, too. I love her with all my heart, just as I love Faith."

Squirming to get away from Theda, Naomi stretched out her chubby arms and spoke a new word Verity's way. *"Mamm, mamm."*

The look of love in the child's eyes and her

words pushed back the last of the protective walls she had built around her heart. "I am your *mudder*, little one. I always will be."

Theda studied Verity's face. "And Leviticus? What of him, child?" The older, wiser woman reached for her hand and patted it. "He is your husband now. Is he in your heart to stay? Will you let him be the husband you longed for all those years ago?"

Verity had to be honest. She couldn't be a Plain woman of faith and continually lie. "I'm ashamed to say my heart is still closed to him, even in this time of stress."

"It makes me to wonder if Albert's regained health and time won't heal the problems you two are dealing with. Leviticus's past life is over, sweet one. It's time to move on. You both have *kinner* depending on you. Find your way back to each other. There is much to be done on the grove. Leviticus will need your support and affection to make it through these hard times."

Verity lowered her head, condemned. She meant it when she promised, "I will pray for

Gott to put a strong love in my heart for Leviticus. I promise."

"You know we're all praying *Gott*'s will for Albert." She released Verity's hand. "Accept His will, child. What will be, will be…no matter how much you want otherwise." Theda's smile deepened. "Now, get some rest and make sure you keep an eye on Clara. She's walking like she's ready to drop that *boppli* any moment."

"I will." She took Naomi from Theda's arms and snuggled her close as she walked back to the house, leaving Leviticus to his own devices. Her head on Verity's shoulder, Naomi took a long, deep breath and closed her eyes, whispering, *"Mamm."*

"*Ya, boppli.* I am your *mamm*. *Gott* has brought us together. We are a *familye*."

The last of family and friends said their goodbyes, leaving Verity alone in the house with Clara and the children. She didn't have a clue where Leviticus was at that moment. She knew he was upset about something.

She silently prayed for him, asking *Gott* to bring peace to his mind.

Ten minutes later, Verity eased into a kitchen chair, her fingers reaching into her hair and pulling out the pins securely holding her prayer covering in place. It had been a long, grueling day. She needed a moment to herself. Time to think about what Theda had said.

Smiling, Clara placed her hand on the small of her back as she leaned against the kitchen's worn porcelain sink. "The girls drift off?"

"*Ya.* Finally." Verity observed her sister-in-law, looking for signs of labor. Seeing none, she eased back in her chair and took in a calming breath. "Faith wanted to stay up and wait for her new *daed*'s return, but I persuaded her tomorrow morning would be soon enough." She stretched out her legs, wishing she was in a nice hot bath full of scented bubbles, one of her secret indulgences. "That child's so excited to have Leviticus in her life. She loves having him as her new *daed*."

Her hand still pressed to her back, Clara's brow crinkled into a heavy frown. "Makes me wonder where he could be. Ain't so? It's coming on dark. Why isn't he home with his *familye*?" She finished drying her hands on the tea towel as she spoke and then placed the cloth by the sink.

Verity didn't want to admit it, but she knew Clara was right. Where had Leviticus gone? He did have a family who needed him home. "His leaving like this happens too often. He becomes so quiet and distant at times, especially since Albert fell ill, and now that Albert is showing remarkable signs of improvement he's still too quiet." She smiled over at Clara. "Oh, I know he has a lot on his mind, but I'm concerned whatever is troubling him is more than just rebuilding the grove."

"He didn't take the truck or any of his things, did he?" Clara pulled out a chair across from Verity and eased down into it.

She slipped off her shoes, arched her swollen feet and splayed out her toes in relief. With gusto, she fanned her face with her apron, the movement causing damp wisps of hair around her face to dance.

Verity struggled to keep her composure. They'd had such a *gut* morning. What could have happened? "*Nee*, I checked a moment ago." Her finger traced the shape of a rose imprinted on the tablecloth. "The vehicle is where he left it last night, his clothes in the drawers." Images of Leviticus walking away from his Amish life minutes after the dirt was shoveled on his mother's simple casket snaked through her again. *What if Albert dies? Will he run again? Faith will be devastated.* And how would she feel? "Only *Gott* knows where he is." Verity managed to hold the threatening tears in check.

Clara sucked in her breath and paused a moment before pushing in the kitchen chair she'd been sitting in. Its legs scraping against the wood floor brought Verity back to the present.

Clara sighed and put her arm around Verity's shoulders. "I'll be praying for you, my dearest friend." She glanced at the clock on the wall. "But I really must go. Now that we're moving back into our own home, Solomon expects me to be there, waiting for him to finish arranging furniture back into its place. A half hour ago, I told him I was only coming back into the *haus* to collect my dishes." Her gentle smile turned into laughter. She slipped her swollen feet back into her church shoes and touched Verity once more on the shoulder. "You're sure you are all right?"

"Yes, I'm sure." Verity rose.

"*Gut.* Now try to get some rest. You look worse than I do and I'm nine months gone." Clara chuckled, lines mapping her forehead. "Those circles under your eyes get darker every time I see you. You mustn't let the children run you ragged. You know I'm only a phone call away."

Verity wanted to blurt out it wasn't the children keeping her awake and overwrought at night. It was Leviticus, too, their sudden arranged marriage…her growing feelings for him. But she kept silent. Tonight would be soon enough to cry into her pillow if Leviticus didn't return. "God's will be done, *ya*?"

Clara nodded with a smile, lifting her basket containing ovenware. A second in time and she was slumped over, the basket dropped back on the counter with a clatter.

Verity hurried over. "What's wrong? Are you in pain?"

A smile danced on Clara's lips. "I think my labor's finally started. I've been feeling nagging little twinges all day. They're getting stronger and more painful."

"This is one of your pranks, isn't it? You're just saying that to get my mind off Leviticus."

Clara sucked in her breath. "*Nee*, these pains are no joke. This is the real thing."

"And you said nothing to me? Does Solomon know?" Verity led Clara over to the chair she'd just vacated and eased her down.

"*Nee*, I didn't tell him. He was needed at Chicken John's and I let him go. This is our first *kind*. There's plenty of time to fetch him." Clara sucked in a breath and grimaced, her pains renewed.

Verity glanced at the clock, prepared to time the next onset of birthing pains. She hovered, unsure what to do, but knowing she had better get in touch with Solomon, and fast. She didn't want to scare Clara, but if her pains had been coming regularly all day, she might well need to reach the midwife urgently. "He'd want to know you might be in labor."

"I thought there was plenty of time and Chicken John really needed his help. They're growing old, he and Ulla." Clara flashed a quick smile at Verity that fast turned into a painful scowl. Clara didn't have a chance to comment further. Her head dropped, a groan emanating from her dry lips. She bent forward, her arms encircling her middle in misery.

"Does Solomon have his work phone with him?"

Clara's head bobbed. Her back rose slightly as she took in a long, deep cleansing breath as the pain receded. "I saw him slip it in his trouser pocket this morning."

Verity searched for the grove's business phone in the kitchen drawer. "Stay calm. I'm calling him and then the midwife." Thinking back to Faith's birth, Verity remembered how her precious *boppli* arrived with little fanfare.

"Please let him answer," she prayed aloud as she dialed on the small black cell phone kept for emergencies.

A light in the kitchen told Leviticus that Verity was still up. He slowed his steps, considered what kind of mood she might be in since he'd walked off hours ago. He'd needed time to himself, time to pray and confess his hidden sins.

Ready to face whatever she had waiting for him, he sprang up the steps, opened the back door, only to stop midstep. Verity had her arms around Clara, assisting her across the kitchen floor.

"What's happened? Is she okay?" He took off his sweaty straw hat and tossed it on the kitchen table.

Verity glanced his way, her expression a mixture of stark terror and relief. "She's in labor. Solomon's across town at Chicken John's. No one's answering their phones." A quick glance directed at Clara had Verity moving again. "I called the midwife, but she can't come. She's busy birthing another *boppli*, so Clara's going to have to go to the hospital."

"Give her to me." Leviticus's big hands visibly shook as he reached out for Clara. "Keep trying to reach Solomon. I've got my truck outside. I'll take her to the hospital."

"But you're covered in mud." Verity shielded Clara from him like the pregnant woman had no say in the matter.

He paused and watched Verity vacillate between relief that he'd offered an immediate solution and revulsion at the thought of Clara riding in his bumpy truck all the way to Memorial hospital.

"If you have a better idea, spit it out."

Clara made a valiant attempt to stifle a groan, but they both heard her cry.

"Look, it's me and my truck, or you're delivering this baby. What's it going to be?"

Verity flinched at his words. "Do you want to go with him?"

Clara nodded. "I'll go." And then her face flushed a bright red. "I think my water just broke."

Three heads looked down at the kitchen floor. A puddle of pink liquid formed around their feet.

"Let's get going." Leviticus lifted Clara into his arms. "Tell Solomon to meet us at the hospital." He hurried for the back door with Clara in tow.

Am I crazy? He'd never delivered a baby before but could if he had to. He'd delivered a breech-birthed goat while in Afghanistan, but he wasn't thinking about *that* birth right now. He was thinking about what Solomon would do to him if he let anything happen to his beloved Clara and their first child.

Verity turned on the porch light and held the screen door open wide, but she didn't speak again until he ran down the wooden steps with Clara bouncing as he took them two at a time. "Be gentle with her, but hurry. I don't think she has much time to spare."

He turned his head. Concern strained Verity's face, but she managed a sweet smile for him. He held her gaze for a heartbeat, longing to reassure her. Tucking Clara into the front seat, he slammed the door and hurried up the steps to Verity. "I promise you, she and the baby will be all right." He pulled her close, felt her trembling body and put a light kiss on her cheek. "Don't fret, *fraa*. Clara will be fine. Trust me."

Verity held his gaze, her eyes sparkling as he let her go and she moved toward the door. "I do trust you." Her words came out firm and clear, convincing him she meant it, but then he noticed her right hand. It gripped the screen door so hard all the blood had drained from her fingers. She didn't trust him. Not with Clara, and certainly never with her heart.

Ignoring his own misery, he called out, "Make that call to Solomon." His boots crunched on the gravel as he rushed back toward the truck, but he heard his *fraa*'s encouraging words.

"Go with *Gott*, Leviticus. Trust in Him. He'll see you through."

Chapter Fifteen

Even with his heavy trousers and long-sleeved shirt, the cold hospital air swept around him like an arctic breeze, chilling him to the bone. He knew they kept the temperature down to keep germs at bay, but he was miserably cold, his hands like ice.

The plastic chair he sat in creaked as he shoved his hands under his thighs, seeking a measure of warmth. No doubt Solomon would find a reason to make all this his fault, even though he had no control over Clara's labor or when it started.

She'd been in a lot of pain when they'd first arrived at the hospital. A nurse had whisked her up to labor and delivery. He'd hurried along behind the stretcher, forgotten by both chattering nurses until they had reached their destination.

One nurse turned toward him, blocking his entrance. Her name tag read Jessica. "You're the father?"

"No, the brother-in-law."

"You can't come in." A grimace lifted her narrow lips.

"But—"

She pointed to a chair just outside the door. "Sit there. We'll call for you if you're needed," and then firmly shut the door in his face.

Leviticus looked around for a men's magazine or local newspaper. Nothing, though he had plenty to read if he enjoyed women's magazines.

Bored, his thoughts wandered to places normally forbidden. He regretted he hadn't been at Naomi's birth. His unit had been on a six-month deployment to Afghanistan while Julie was still pregnant. No one had asked him if it was convenient or still fit into his life's plan. He'd had to go and ended up making do with Julie's housekeeper Skyping him about his child's birth. She'd muttered he had a daughter. When he asked questions, he got little more than "She's doing well." Her last sentence to him had been, "Do you have a name picked out for your daughter?" He'd replied, "Naomi," but wasn't sure she'd even heard him before the connection was severed.

He scrubbed at the itchy growth on his chin, changed position and crossed his legs. There were a lot of things he'd done wrong in his life, but Julie's pregnancy had been his biggest mess-up yet. He'd enjoyed his army life and all the perks that had come with it, like most young men did when they were irresponsible. Not that he would change anything if he could. Naomi was his blood, his heart.

And look at me now. Married to a woman who doesn't want to be married to me and forced to watch her make the best of a bad situation. What a fool you are, Leviticus Hilty. Ruining first your life and now Verity's.

In the past, always pleasant and in control of her emotions, Verity hadn't tried to hide her contempt for him his first few days home. And he didn't blame her for objecting to Otto's marriage plans. No woman, Amish or *Englisch*, liked the prospect of marrying a man they hadn't chosen. *Certainly not someone like me.* Amish women expected their husbands to be in charge. Strong. Men of faith. He had to admit, after their quick wedding, her attitude had softened some for appearance's sake, but moments alone with her convinced him she resented the marriage.

He huffed, then remembered he had things to be grateful for, too. This evening when he'd checked in on his *daed*, his father had been pink-skinned and looked stronger. They'd taken him off oxygen, were feeding him more than just Jell-O and watery soup. The nurse explained the doctors expected him to live and make a reasonable recovery, but she had made it clear he would need in-home care when he left the hospital. Verity couldn't manage Albert on her own with two children to see to. Leviticus would need to find an agency who provided twenty-four-hour care or ask the community for help.

He chewed at his nail, a habit he thought he'd gotten rid of months after leaving Afghanistan, but it periodically resurfaced thanks to his remaining PTSD.

He glanced at the clock on the wall. It showed only a half hour had passed since he'd last looked at it.

He saw movement in his peripheral vision and witnessed Solomon's arrival and interaction with the desk nurse. Their eyes met. His brother's weary expression, the way the man's body was bent over told him Solomon's day had been a hard one.

"She's in there." He pointed to the door across the hall where he'd been keeping sentry.

Solomon nodded. "*Danki* for bringing her, Leviticus. And for keeping watch."

Without another word, Solomon rushed into his wife's room and shut the door behind him.

Clara had her beloved Solomon with her now. He'd best be heading home. He needed to let Verity know everything was under control, and that his father was better. He rose and stretched his aching body. He looked down first one length of the hall and then the other.

Clara's door opened, and Solomon shuffled out. "They ran me off. Said they'd call me back in when it was time." He gave a mirthless laugh. "I think they thought I would pass out on them or something."

Solomon did look decidedly green. Leviticus sat and patted the seat next to him. "I'm not surprised they would think that. You look awful, ready to fall."

Solomon crossed the hall and took the chair Leviticus offered him, his knees splayed out, elbows braced on the armrests. "I am tired. There's so much to be done on the grove, but Chicken John's place is devastated. Ulla went to stay with Mose and Sarah." He rubbed his eyes, lifted his head. "The whole community felt the punch of the storm."

"Otto said people will be coming down from the North to help."

"*Ya*, there'll be a busload tonight and more able-bodied men on their way tomorrow." He finally looked Leviticus in the eye. "We need all the help we can get on the grove." He raked his hand, covered in mud, through his mussed brown hair. "He really wants you to stay, Leviticus."

"I know. I'm a married man now, with responsibilities. I need the grove to support my family as much as you do." He placed his hand on his brother's thigh. "You have to know…things are different now. I want to succeed and come to trust *Gott*, be a *bruder* you can be proud of."

Solomon shook his head, confusion lowering his brows. "I've never understood why you left. Why abandon *Daed* and the grove when they needed you most? *Mamm*'s death almost finished *Daed* off ten years ago. He really struggled with both those losses. Time and age have worn him down. His first stroke took a lot out of him. I thought this second big one would kill him." Solomon's piercing gaze seemed to look deep inside Leviticus's soul, searching out the truth.

Talking about his mother's death, about the stress he'd put on her, was a subject Leviticus always avoided. But giving Solomon an explanation for his leaving was long overdue. "When *Mamm* died, I guess a piece of me died with her." Leviticus shifted uncomfortably in the plastic chair.

Only his father knew what was in his heart, why he'd left, and even then, not all the truth had come out as they'd talked. "I watched Mom kill herself with hard work. She took care of everyone but herself." He rubbed his hand across the stubble growing on his chin. "*Daed* let her die from hard work, and I helped kill her by acting like a fool and shaming her." He blinked back a tear.

"I should have stopped my running around. *Daed* should have made her slow down."

Solomon sat up straight in his chair, his expression bemused, eyebrows knitting together. "Your childish shenanigans and hard work didn't kill her, *bruder.* Cancer did."

It was the first time Leviticus had heard the word *cancer* associated with his mother. Even his *dat* had kept silent. *She'd had cancer?* "What do you mean she had cancer? Someone would have told me."

"*Nee, bruder.* I only know because I overheard *Mamm* and *Daed* talking about the doctors' diagnosis when they thought we were out doing chores. Years later, I admitted to *Daed* I knew about the cancer. It pained him that I knew. He explained the illness wasn't allowed to be talked about to anyone. It was *Mamm* who insisted it remain a secret, and *Daed* complied." Solomon wiped a tear from his cheek. "Her kind of cancer was terrible, cruel and aggressive. She'd ignored the signs, left it too long."

Fury rose up. Leviticus wrung his hands,

flexing his fingers that felt stiff with rage. "I should have been told. You were my *bruder*. You could have told me sooner."

"I was afraid of how you'd react. You were just a *bu*, her youngest. I wasn't much older. She tried to spare us. Don't go looking for someone to blame."

Leviticus ducked his head. His mother had tried to shield him every day of his life. Was that why it had taken a war, the horror of battle to screw his head on right, to bring him to a full understanding of what was important and what could be easily set aside?

Leviticus looked hard at Solomon, needing to be angry with someone. "You should have told me when I came home."

"Maybe. But I did as she asked. Not even the community knew. When she passed suddenly, people thought it was from a heart attack or stroke. No one asked. Her secret was kept to the end."

Leviticus shook his head, tears running down his face. His brother's embrace came out of nowhere. Leviticus held on for dear life and cried like a child as they rocked together, all the bitterness and strife between them ebbing away.

A woman in scrubs stood just outside Clara's room. "Mr. Hilty! Your wife is calling for you. She's ready to push." She disappeared again, leaving the door slightly ajar.

Leviticus pulled away, sniffed. "Sounds like that baby's wanting to meet his *daed*."

Solomon scrubbed the last tears from his eyes. "I best be getting back." He rose, hesitated and then turned back to Leviticus. "You'll be going home to Verity? She must be a basket of nerves by now. She could use a strong shoulder to lean on."

"*Ya*, I'm going home."

Solomon disappeared behind the shut door, but not before he shot a big grin Leviticus's way.

Cancer? Leviticus sat for a moment, thinking about what he'd just learned about their mother's passing, about the man he needed to become now that he knew the truth. He could change. *Lord, for Verity's sake, help me be the best husband I can be.* Even as he thought the words, he wondered, would Verity ever forgive him for leaving her? Could he be Amish Plain for the rest of his life, or would he keep running from life's hard trials? He shrugged. Now things were different. He wanted to change. To be Amish in mind and deed, but only time would tell if that was possible.

Verity vigorously washed her two daughters' late-night milk glass and sippy cup and placed both upside down on the drain-cloth next to the sink. The stray cat she'd brought into the house knocked one of Faith's books off the children's tiny table and chair set, making her jump.

Why was Clara's labor taking so long? Word should have come by now. The woman was young, healthy. Complications in childbirth were rare these days, especially when a doctor was in attendance, but they did happen. *Nothing's impossible.*

Verity dried her hands, chastising herself.

That's foolish talk. Clara's fine. The boppli*'s fine. You're just a worrier.*

The roar of Leviticus's old truck coming to a stop in the side yard had Verity abandoning the cup of coffee she'd picked up. She rushed to the back door and flipped on the outside light. A yellow glow lit the darkness. *He's taking a long time coming in.*

As though she had wings on her feet, she rushed out onto the back porch and watched as he turned the corner of the house and strolled toward her. *Does he have to walk so slow?* His head down, she couldn't search his face for a hint of news. Illuminated by the porch light now, his mud-splattered clothes reminded her that he'd had a hard day. A long night. *Had he eaten supper? He must be bone tired.*

Instead of bounding up the steps, he took them one by one. Her heart beat faster. Pumped hard. Adrenaline coursed through her body. But then she saw his wide smile, the look of joy in his eyes. *Hallelujah! All is well. The* boppli *is here.*

He reached the top step and she grabbed for his hand, yanking him up onto the porch with her excitement. "Well. Don't just stand there with a silly grin. Tell me. Is it a *bu* or girl? What does it weigh? Does it favor Clara or Solomon?"

He laughed at her, the sound of his joy deep and robust.

A thrill rushed through her. She remembered that laugh from years ago. *Best not think of those times.* "Talk to me, before I wring the facts from your scrawny neck."

He laughed, but remained quiet until he stepped into the kitchen, leaving the door open for Verity to pass through. "I hung around for a while in case Solomon needed me, and then a nurse finally told me Clara was fine and that I had a niece. I have no idea who she looks like or how much she weighs. I didn't stick around once I caught a peek of the baby being pushed to the nursery in a plastic cart. You'll have to wait till tomorrow and see for yourself."

"A girl!" Verity's face lifted toward the

heavens. "Thank You, Jesus, for the answered prayer." She couldn't hold back the wave of laughter that swept over her. In her joy, Verity forgot to be reserved. She squeezed Leviticus's hand hard. His eyes enlarged with what had to be surprise. Tonight, she was deliriously happy, brave enough to touch him again. She longed to be held in his arms, so they could rejoice together as a husband and wife would.

"Did she say what they were calling the *boppli*? Did she have an easy time of it?" She didn't wait for him to answer her questions. "A girl! Oh, I'm so glad," she repeated, joyously laughing at her own foolish behavior. Renewed hope coursed through her for the first time in weeks. "Clara wanted a girl so much. She can show her off at the Thanksgiving dinner."

Verity remembered she was holding Leviticus's hand and dropped it. She stepped back, letting him slip past. "Come, sit. Have coffee with me while you tell me everything you know."

Pulling out a chair, he obediently accepted her offer of a hot drink. "There's not much to tell. I sat in a hard chair for hours. It was cold enough in that hospital to hang meat. No one spoke—"

Verity whirled around from the kitchen counter, the spoon of sugar she'd been about to add to his coffee mug suspended in midair. "Just tell me what you know. What you saw. I want to hear everything...about Clara, the *boppli*." She would never understand men if she lived to be a hundred. Why were they so closemouthed?

Leviticus scooted over to a plate of freshly baked chocolate-chip cookies and shoved one in his mouth. Another quickly followed.

He hasn't eaten. I should have offered to heat him a plate of food. Guilt plagued her, but first she wanted information. She'd feed the silent man once he'd told her everything.

Eating a third cookie, he spoke around it. "No one told me if there was a problem." He shoved another cookie in his mouth.

Verity moved to the refrigerator and pulled

out cold chops and sweet potato casserole. Leviticus hated marshmallows. She grinned at the thought of him having to eat around them. "Now, tell me about the *kind.* Is she dirty-blond like Solomon or brown-haired like Clara? Is she plump or all legs and arms?" She put a fat chop on his plate and scooped out a heaping serving of sweet potato casserole.

"From what I could see, she didn't seem to have much meat on her, and not much hair for that matter. All I know is…the *boppli* looked like a *boppli* swaddled in a blanket. You have to remember, I've never seen one as young as this before, and the nurse had her wrapped tight, like a mummy in a blanket."

Verity's brow arched in surprise. "But surely you were at Naomi's birth. Don't you remember how she looked?" Verity slid the plate of food into the heated oven and then yanked out a chair across from him to wait for the food to heat.

When he didn't respond, she looked his

way. His hands clenched the back of the kitchen chair, and she noticed his face had blanched paper white. *I knew it. Something is wrong.* "What is it? There's something you're not telling me." She touched his shoulder. His body was trembling.

"Sit down, Verity." He cleared his voice, took a gulp of the coffee she'd handed him moments before.

Her eyes held him captive. She didn't want to sit. She wanted to scream. "Is it Clara? The *boppli*?"

A frown pinched his forehead. "No. It's not them. I told you. They're fine." His Adam's apple bobbed as he swallowed hard. "It's me. There are things you don't know about me. It's time you did."

Verity remained standing, but her legs suddenly threatened to buckle under her. "What kinds of things, Leviticus? You're scaring me."

His shoulders stiffened. "I wasn't at Naomi's birth. I didn't see her until she was almost six months old."

"But you said—"

"No, I never said I was there. You assumed I was." His eyes turned a dark blue. So dark she could see her own reflection in them. "Look. We're both tired. It's late. Tonight's not the right time to talk about all this. I should have seen it was the wrong time to dump this on you." He moved away from the table, his head down. "I'll see you in the morning."

Verity watched her new husband leave the room, his meal forgotten. What secrets was he holding on to? Would he ever confide in her? She ran her hand across the table, brushed a few cookie crumbs into her hand. She'd wait awhile, approach him about this conversation when things were more settled.

Lord, I need Your help reaching Leviticus. Please bless me with the right words when he does talk to me. Don't let me mess up our future. I want to be a gut fraa.

Chapter Sixteen

Both busy with their own work, two days slipped past uneventfully. Life went on. Leviticus said nothing about the night Clara's *boppli* was born. She held her questions about his past for another occasion. Verity looked at the back door for the third time in five minutes and forced herself to stop.

Get a grip on yourself, bensel. *He'll come in from the grove when he's hungry, and not a moment sooner.*

Her stomach went all funny at the thought of seeing him, talking to him, like there was a hive of honeybees taking up residence in her insides.

Her resentment toward him was changing subtly but it was still there, just not as intense. He'd been trapped into this loveless marriage, too. Little by little, she'd begun to make allowances when he grew quiet, to show kindness instead of anger, even though she knew he was as frustrated as her. He'd responded in kind and treated her fairly. Showed affection to her, not just to the *kinner*. He smiled more, the sound of his laugh thrilling her unexpectedly at times.

The day before, she worked in the yard and found herself seeking him out like some lovesick teen.

Verity jumped back when the bacon she'd been cooking spit hot grease her way. It had never been in her nature to distrust, but she wouldn't be fooled by Leviticus again. She was a grown woman now, fully aware of how real love felt. A man who loves his *fraa* shows his love. His emotions made him smile a certain way at his woman.

But he smiled at you that way this morning. You'd be lying if you said he hadn't.

She shrugged her shoulders, refocusing on turning the last thick slice of bacon and transferring it to an absorbent stack of paper towels. She wasn't going to let her growing interest in Leviticus cause her to have a bad day. Nee, *never again. My joy is in the Lord.*

Breaking a dozen eggs for scrambling, she found herself smiling at the sound of Naomi's giggles, enjoying the way her young *kind* chattered away in her own mysterious language to Faith.

She jumped and dropped the serving fork when the back door suddenly opened. Leviticus trudged in, dirt covering his face and hands. The straw hat on his sweaty head sat at a jaunty angle, like the wind had caught and displaced it.

He glanced her way, half smiled and then kissed both girls on the cheek. Naomi gave him a toothy grin, but Faith giggled and snuck in a kiss of her own on his grizzled face.

Verity watched as he turned on his heel, not speaking a word to her. Showers were predicted again, but later in the day. Had the news put him in a foul mood? It didn't take much to make him moody since he'd returned.

He moved over to the kitchen sink and splashed water on his face and neck. She stifled a gasp as he used her clean dish towel to dry himself off. If his *mamm* had been alive, she would have sent him away from the table for such disrespect, but Verity didn't have the heart to utter a complaint. The man looked too worn out to say a word. *Had he and Solomon had words again?*

"The *kinner* ate oatmeal and blueberries, but if you want fresh eggs, there's some made."

He looked at her, nodded and ruffled Faith's hair as he took his seat. "*Ya*, eggs sound fine."

She poured him a mug of coffee and set it down in front of him. He grabbed the cup and downed the drink—black and bitter, without a drop of milk or sugar. Her shoulders shuddered in distaste. She wasn't sure what to say to him in his mood. “How’s the grove coming along?”

“We need more workers.” His words were crisp, with an edge that had nothing to do with her. He was worried, tired and hungry for a hot meal.

Verity dished up a plate of freshly made toast, scrambled eggs and crispy bacon and tried to remember how to use the small microwave Leviticus had brought home the night before. She concentrated on how to start the newfangled gadget. She didn’t hear him walk up behind her until he spoke close to her ear.

“Just put the plate in, cover the food with a paper towel and punch in the amount of warming time you want. Heating this shouldn’t take more than a few seconds.” His finger pointed to a red square button that screamed *START*.

She thought she’d remembered his instructions from the night before, but suddenly his hand was next to hers, moving it away, punching in numbers. She jerked at his touch. *Why does he have lightning in his fingers?* Frustrated, she flushed. *Does he notice how prickly I am when he touches me?*

His smile at her was easy. "If you cook the food too long, it gets rock hard or burns." A bell went off and he opened the microwave door. "Look, thirty seconds was all the eggs needed."

"Are you sure Otto will approve of this contraption? I know of no other Amish who have one."

"Ach. Do you think Otto cares if you have an added convenience? He's bought one for his office."

Faith pushed in close, gawking at the steaming plate of eggs and bacon. "Can you warm mine, too?"

"*Ya*, sure. Hand it to me." She looked back toward Leviticus, who was pulling out a chair to sit in.

"Danki," she muttered and then pressed her mouth shut. It was obvious Leviticus needed peace and quiet. The beeper sounded

again, and she opened the microwave door, surprised her plate wasn't hot to the touch. Being introduced to new *Englischer* contraptions always made Verity edgy and feel a bit stupid. She tucked the dirty hand towel in her apron band and scooted away.

Leviticus took a huge bite of his eggs and shoved a whole slice of bacon into his mouth.

She sat at the table, her nervous fingers smoothing out her apron, avoiding Leviticus's gaze. "Otto told me your church classes began last week."

"*Ya*, kind of the cart before the horse. I've got another session with Mose this afternoon." He picked up his fork and shoveled in another mouthful of eggs. "He gave me some pamphlets to look at. They were interesting."

"So you're ready?"

"Ready?"

She grabbed Naomi's hand as it reached out to grab a handful of bacon. "*Ya*, to become a Plain man in every sense of the word?"

His head bobbed. “As ready as I’ll ever be.”

Verity pushed her food around the plate. *I certain-sure hope so.*

“I forgot to tell you. I bought you something else.”

Verity glanced over at Leviticus as he polished off the last of his food. His eyes sparkled with something akin to mischief. “What is it? Not another microwave.” She forced a laugh. What was the man up to?

Leviticus returned her smile. “*Nee.* Just something you’ve been needing with two children to raise.” He put out his hand toward her and she hesitantly took it, enjoying the feel of the calluses on his palm that he’d earned from hard work on the grove. His fingers wrapped tight around her hand for a quick moment, making her breath quicken. She pulled her hand away and lifted Naomi out of her high chair and motioned for Faith to follow. “*Komm!*” Leviticus took her hand again.

Out the kitchen and across the back porch he held her hand. Faith jumped each step, singing as she swung about her big gray bunny that her new *daed* had brought her home days before.

The door of the shed creaked as Leviticus opened it, then pulled the light string as he went. Light flooded the small storage room. Verity gasped when she saw the white washing machine and matching dryer bathed in artificial light. “You bought me *Englischer* appliances?” Her heart beat against her chest. What would *Gott* think? What would Otto have to say?

Reading her expression, Leviticus said, “Otto knows all about the purchase. I asked his permission and he liked the idea so much he bought a set for Theda the same day.”

“But these things are for *Englisch*, not us Amish.”

“They’re for whoever needs them, Verity. And you need one. That old contraption you wash on needs to be slung on the metal heap. I don’t see how it’s lasted this long.”

“But—”

“There’s no shame in using what is provided to us by *Gott*'s ingenuity. Our community *Ordnung* rules allow for the use of electricity in Pinecraft." Leviticus opened the lid of the washer and motioned for her to come look.

"But a washer?" Verity peered in. A massive tub waited for clothes to be thrown in. "Doesn't this thing need water to work?"

"It does. The plumber is coming in an hour or so, and so is the electrician. You should be able to use these by tomorrow at the latest."

"I don't know what to say," she muttered. And she didn't. She didn't know how she felt with such an *Englischer* machine to do her washing. And what would others in the community say? Would there be suggestions that Leviticus was dragging her into the *Englischer* world?

Leviticus pulled out a booklet and several papers from the inside of the machine and began flipping through its pages. "Let's see how this thing works."

Reading out loud to himself, Leviticus

made his way back to the porch, Faith running by his heels. Verity shut the shed door, her mind in a whirl. She was used to the simple life. This machine felt like an intrusion into her way of living, but if Otto had bought one for Theda, how could she complain? Cell phones, microwaves and now washers. Where would it all end?

She followed Leviticus into the house, Naomi riding on her hip. She marched on, perplexed and fighting down the joy bubbling up in her. Not for the washer, but that Leviticus had thought of her, considered her needs. She wasn't used to this new man she called her husband, but she wasn't complaining, either. Not for a moment. Joining the church, committing to *Ordnung* classes proved to her that Leviticus was dedicated to change. Now, if they could just learn to love and trust one another.

Tired, Leviticus held the door for Otto and Mose Fischer, and then followed them into the church. He'd dealt with two long days and nights working in the grove but made time for his condensed *Ordnung* classes to please Verity, like joining the church and being baptized the Sunday after they'd been married had managed to do. The community's *Ordnung* rules were important to her, so they were important to him now, too.

His first session with Mose had been surprisingly interesting. Why hadn't he seen that the *Ordnung* rules were fair back when he was young, that they were put in place to help the people of Pinecraft, not control them? *Was I too young? Too rebellious?* Rules kept the faithful prospering. He'd have no problem living within the boundaries set down by Bishop Otto Fischer and the pastors.

As they walked out of the church together, Mose rubbed at the bridge of his nose. He paused. "There'll be another group of men coming to the grove tomorrow. Seven thirty too early for your family?"

Leviticus laughed. "*Nee.* Verity and I are up before the chickens nowadays. With all your kids, I'm pretty sure you and Sarah know all about early-morning feedings and messy breakfast tables."

"Sarah and I have six rambunctious *kinner*." Mose looked down and picked at a dried clump of dirt on his trousers. "She's been feeling poorly of late. This pregnancy's been hard on her."

Seven children! How did Sarah manage? Yet, every time he saw Mose's *fraa* she looked happy, fresh as a spring flower and not in the least stressed.

Verity came to mind. He pictured her heavy with his *kind*. How would she feel about having *kinner* in the future? Not that there was much of a chance of that happening. Their marriage was in name only.

For a while now, he'd known he still had serious feelings for Verity. Feelings that went far beyond appreciation and friendship. Being realistic, he also knew there was no way she would feel the same about him after she learned what he'd done during the war. And he planned to tell her someday soon. He had to.

"You two getting along okay?" Mose climbed onto his bike and straddled it, distracting Leviticus's daydreaming.

"We're getting there. Ours was an arranged marriage, you know. It'll probably take time to get to know each other again. Eventually, all the kinks will be ironed out."

Mose smiled. "I know what you mean. My marriage was one of convenience, too." He laughed, his head thrown back as he hooted. "I quickly learned my Sarah, the mildest woman you can find, has a sharp tongue when riled." He nodded, lifting his suspender strap as it slipped off his shoulder. "She's a *gut* woman, and the best *mamm*, especially to Beatrice, our strong-willed *dochder*. Sarah's smart and knows just how to handle that tiny replica of Ulla."

Mose and Leviticus snorted at the reference to Ulla. Most men in Pinecraft felt sorry for Chicken John, but Leviticus had noticed the man seemed happy enough with his choice of wife.

"What's so funny?" Otto came out of the church and locked the door behind them.

"My comment about Ulla," Mose said with a smile for his father, and got a knowing grin back.

"Like us, Chicken John can't live without his woman, but enough of this silly chitchat about the womenfolk. My supper's waiting in the oven and a man needs his nourishment if he's to get a good night's sleep."

After waving the two men off, Leviticus rode his bike slow and easy through the streets of Pinecraft, becoming familiar with the houses going up, the new hotel being built in the center of the community.

A brisk wind almost blew him off his bike. Fall was here, and Thanksgiving would be coming soon. All the vacant-rooms and for-rent signs would disappear quickly enough. Spare rooms always filled up fast during the fall and winter months, when the snowbirds and Northern Amish began to come down to enjoy a bit of warm Florida sunshine.

Leviticus was disappointed to still see plenty of damage that had been caused by the hurricane. It would take months, maybe years, for Pinecraft to get back to what it had been, but the community was hard at work, preparing as best they could for the crowd of visitors arriving by bus daily.

Turning down the gravel road to the grove, his *daed*'s improved health came to mind.

He hoped his *daed* would be pleasantly pleased at how much work he and Solomon had been able to agree on and get done. The doctors were promising Albert would be home as early as Thanksgiving week. He smiled, picking up speed. *I hope they're right.*

His stress level was down to a manageable number of late. He had Verity's kindness and good humor to thank for being able to settle down into a calm routine. The only time his hands shook now was when he and Verity momentarily disagreed, which hadn't been as often lately and was always his fault. In fact, there were times Verity seemed almost friendly, like she'd stopped resenting their marriage quite so much. Sometimes he caught her looking at him, her gaze still elusive, but warmer and hopefully full of unspoken promises.

He still needed to talk to her about the war, his PTSD and what all that entailed, but he was in no hurry to bring up the subjects and spoil what progress they'd made. Her knowing about his fighting in the war might put a rift between them, and he didn't want that. Would she trust him around the girls after she learned what a fool he'd been? Her questions would be hard to answer, reminders of what he'd done. What would she think of him once she'd heard everything?

Chapter Seventeen

Still apprehensive but thrilled with Leviticus's surprise of a new washer and dryer, Verity waited for the *Englisch* men to install water and electricity to the shed before she'd go out with a basket of dirty clothes. Sitting down with a cup of leftover coffee, Verity glanced over the machine's manuals one more time, shaking her head in confusion.

The *Englischers*' new technology was mind-blowing. What in the world had he brought home? Mixed emotions curled her toes in her shoes.

There was no agitator? How would the

clothes get clean with nothing to swish them around?

Leviticus came into the kitchen wearing a smile. He had a kiss for the girls and a cheerful wave in her direction as she mulled over her predicament. "Would you like another cup of coffee? There's at least a cup left," she offered as she watched him and Naomi play tug-of-war with the *kind*'s favorite toy. His hug for Naomi was, as always, long and loving. It was plain to see the child meant the world to him.

He glanced her way as he ruffled Faith's already messy head of hair. "*Nee*, but thanks. I've got a lot to do today."

She waved him off with a smile, but her thoughts remained on her new husband. He seemed calm this morning, had a slight spring to his step. Almost as if he were happy. Like he'd finally found contentment. Watching as he plodded along, she waved at him as he turned back around and sent the girls a hand-blown kiss. She tried hard to hold down the spurt of joy warming her soul. Leviticus was becoming the man she'd been promised to all those years ago. She wasn't sure if and when she should reveal how much their new friendship meant to her.

Naomi asleep and Faith coloring on the porch, Verity made her way to the shed and upturned a basket of children's clothes into the big machine's tub. Her thoughts were on Leviticus.

Clara followed her out into the shed, kicking a basket of laundry along with her bare foot, her baby safely tucked in her arms. "What's the matter? You're wearing the strangest expression. If I didn't know better, I'd say you were a lovesick fool."

Not ready to confess her growing feelings for Leviticus and how they kept her perplexed, Verity avoided the subject. "Maybe I should use the homemade soap on the *kinner*'s clothes. I keep looking at these funny liquid washing cubes." She held up one of the colorful squares she'd found in a small cardboard box at the bottom of the washer.

"Leviticus would have warned you against

them if he thought they were dangerous." Clara took the tiny soap square from Verity and examined it. Her brows raised, just as confused as Verity. "You know, we'll look complete *bensels* if we break the machine the first week. Best use this soap. It came with the machine."

"You're bound to be right." But still, Verity's stomach gyrated with nerves. *Englischer* things unnerved her, even though Otto had given his consent. *What if the soap doesn't clean well or gives both* kinner *a rash?*

Taking a deep breath, she took the cube back from Clara and dropped it in the slot marked soap that she'd accidently found a moment before. She shut the lid and punched the button for delicate clothes, reserving judgment until the children's clothes were washed. If all went well, she'd allow herself to feel confident with Leviticus's trousers and her dresses next.

Two hours later, after refusing to use the dryer on such a pretty day, she lifted another sheet from her wicker basket, snapped it out and pegged it on the wire line stretching from the garage wall to a T-shaped post stuck in the ground.

The wind caught the damp sheet and smacked her in the face. Placing her *kapp* back in place, she worked her way down the wire clothesline, pegging and grumbling to herself as she went. She missed her old wringer washer. Albert had been kind when she'd first come to work for him and bought it for her convenience, not that the machine ever performed that well. *Why hadn't Leviticus just gotten it fixed?* She would have hung on to the old machine for sentimental reasons, which was silly, considering its flaws, but she was sentimental. She smiled, remembering how many times she'd smashed her finger in the wringer before she got the hang of its peculiarities, but it had run faithfully... until Monday morning, when she'd tried to start it and nothing happened but a terrible groaning and shaking.

Verity sniffed at another damp sheet ready

to be hung. The abnormal smell of store-bought soap tickled her nose. The clothes coming out of the washer seemed clean enough, but still she doubted.

She peeped through the two sheets blowing in the wind. Beyond the concrete sidewalk, Faith rode her bike, her head down like the race-kart driver they'd seen at the community fair the day before.

Naomi squealed in delight, pulling Verity's attention to her youngest daughter playing in the playpen with a pile of old pots and pans. Drool dampened her terry cloth bib and lightweight sweater. There were plenty of soft dolls and cloth blocks in the toy box the girls shared, but the *kind* learning to walk around the playpen preferred kitchenware and mixing bowls as toys. *A born cook?* Perhaps, but she doubted the talent came from Leviticus. He couldn't boil water, much less make a meal. If Naomi had a bent toward culinary arts, it would have had to come from Julie, her birth mother.

Pegging down a pair of Naomi's store-bought onesies, she allowed her thoughts to wander back to Julie, the woman who'd caught Leviticus's eye while he was away. Was it jealously eating at her? He hadn't said much about Naomi's *mamm* other than she was a professional woman who worked an important job for the military. But what he had said didn't make her sound the type who might be found in a hot kitchen, cooking for her family.

Verity's lip curled. *Unless she was cooking one of those fancy gourmet meals I read about at the pediatrician's office.*

After waving at Clara, who stood at the window watching the children's antics, Verity pressed a hand to her back. She was glad her sister-in-law had dropped in to chat this morning. For some reason, Verity had woken in a melancholy mood. She missed Albert. Missed their comradery and friendship. Clara's teasing and laughter was just what she had needed to cheer up and think positive.

She snatched up the last cloth diaper from

her wicker basket. Pegs in her mouth, she looked up, the sounds of a car speeding down the gravel road leading to the compound drawing her interest. Dust and tiny rocks flew behind a fancy red sports car.

"Faith. Quick! Go tell your *Aenti* Clara someone's coming."

Who in the world could this be?

Solomon and Leviticus strolled toward the farmhouse in companionable silence. It had been a long, arduous day. Dirt had been brought in and spread in the small grove where the most damage had been done. The planting of new midsize peach trees was almost finished. They both agreed they would have never gotten this far along if it hadn't been for the local men's continued help. To say they were grateful would have been an understatement.

"*Daed*'s home day after tomorrow."

Solomon nodded, his smile reaching his eyes. "*Ya*, I know. I'm certain-sure he's going to be happy when he sees all the progress made."

A flash of red shining through a row of small orange trees caught Leviticus's eye. He didn't think it probable, but he asked the question anyway. "You know someone who drives a red sports car?"

Solomon stretched his neck, peering over a row of miniature trees. "*Nee*, that's no one I know."

Leviticus shrugged, no longer interested in the car or its driver. Shoulder to shoulder, the brothers walked on, past Verity's line of clothes flapping in the breeze.

Leviticus pulled off his work hat and wiped perspiration from his brow with the sleeve of his sweat-drenched shirt. One of the few things he missed about his *Englischer* clothes was his beat-up baseball cap. It had a built-in sweatband that really worked.

Solomon reached out and playfully popped one of the black suspenders holding up Leviticus's hand-me-down trousers.

"Two can play that game, *bruder*," Leviticus called as he chased Solomon down, both men having to avoid a doll carriage and Faith's swing suspended from a tree limb as they ran. Inches from his target, Leviticus reached out and missed the black elastic suspender stretched taut against his brother's left shoulder.

Laughing, both men ran up the steps and burst through the kitchen's back door, much as they had as boys. Solomon dodged his brother's hand. Leviticus pursued him, not giving up the chase.

If only Mamm *were still alive.* He and Solomon had always gotten into trouble for their exuberant play. He pictured his *mamm* in front of the old range, her face red from the late-summer heat. He could almost hear her voice as she scolded them for running into the house like they were *kinner* again.

His feet still slick with mud, Leviticus skidded to a halt. A man wearing a suit sat at the breakfast table, in a chair nearest the sink. Verity stood transfixed a foot away, her eyes round, her irises a dark shade of emerald green. *Something is wrong.*

The tall man rose, his forehead creased, expressing his disapproval at their behavior. Leviticus approached. Their eyes met and held. This was no country bumpkin. An air of authority clung to the man like the scent of his expensive cologne. Leviticus had seen men like him before in big cities up north. He'd avoided them like the plague.

"Who's this?" he asked Verity. She remained dumbstruck. Silence vibrated through the room until he heard the wail of a young *boppli* crying in earnest at the back of the house. Was it Naomi? *Nee.* The child sounded too young. Perhaps Clara's new daughter, Rose? *But where are Faith and Naomi?*

His hand outstretched, an obligatory smile twisted the stranger's lips. His smart, well-fitted suit told Leviticus their visitor had money—and lots of it.

Verity cleared her throat, fighting to regain her composure. "This is Maxwell Horthorn. He's come to speak to you about Naomi."

Leviticus continued to ignore the man's outstretched hand. It took a moment for him to take in the ramifications of what Verity had said.

"Where are the *kinner*?"

Verity swallowed hard. "Faith is with Clara and her *boppli*." The tone of her voice was too high. Something was very wrong.

Solomon's shoes scuffed the floor as he moved out of the kitchen toward the bedroom, where his wife and child waited.

Leviticus stepped forward. He pulled a kitchen chair out and sat, his legs stretched out in front of him. He knew how to deflate pompous fools. He'd done it enough in the army. *Act like you're not intimidated.* "What about Naomi? Where is she?" His words were for Verity, but his scowling glare never left Maxwell Horthorn's face.

Horthorn lowered his hand but remained standing. "She's with her mother." The man's accent spoke of the islands to the south. Perhaps Jamaica. "I represent the Miami law firm of Zamora, Smith, Landers and Espinoza."

"I'm sure you do."

Leviticus's eyes cut back to Verity. She stood twisting a dishcloth in her hands, her fingers working the fabric, her tortured gaze fixed on the man. He could hear Naomi now. She had begun to whimper and cry out, *"Mamm!"* Her wail of fear sucked the air from his lungs. He stiffened. The floral scent was unmistakable. Chanel. Julie always wore too much.

High heels clicking on hardwood signaled her arrival in the kitchen. He pulled his gaze away from Verity. The one woman in the world who could ruin his daughter's life stood just inside the kitchen. Julie Hernandez. She hadn't changed in the months since he'd seen her. She was still rakish thin.

There was no smile of greeting between the two, just her usual petulant frown and pouting red mouth. She held Naomi in her arms much like a *kind* might carry a rag doll. Not the way a mother should hold her desperately unhappy child.

Naomi reached out her chubby arms to Verity. *"Mamm... Mamm!"*

Verity took a step forward and then stopped as if held by an invisible string. She stood motionless, her arms dropping limp to her sides. Gentle as a lamb, Verity was no match for Julie's annoyed glare.

"What do you want?" He looked her up and down. Out of her military uniform, she wore her usual business attire: a dark slim pencil skirt and lacy blouse meant to give an air of big-city sophistication. Like the fool he had been, he'd fallen for her gentle Southern charm and delicate features, but he'd finally seen through her, though too late. She had already been pregnant with Naomi by the time he was ready to pack his bags.

His hands clenched into fists. He'd take them both on…and the Miami court system if it meant saving his daughter from the likes of Julie. His thoughts swirled with ugly possibilities, making him sick to his stomach. *This isn't supposed to be happening.* Julie had wanted nothing to do with Naomi when she was a baby. What had changed? For the millionth time, he regretted not getting a signed legal document from her relinquishing custody before he'd left Washington with his daughter.

"Still not warm and welcoming, I see." Contempt laced Julie's soft words. Her smile might have turned up her lips, but her eyes were bright and shiny with rage. She'd always liked power games, playing with people like they were bugs until she squashed them under her heel.

"For some reason, I don't feel friendly today." Anger laced Leviticus's voice.

Naomi continued to cry. Julie put the squirming child on her shoulder and rubbed her back, only making the child cry harder.

"She doesn't know you, Julie. Let Verity hold her for a moment and comfort her."

Julie threw back her head and hooted. "Don't be silly. She's fine with me." Her eyes sought out Verity's gaze. "After all, I'm her mother." Julie looked down at the child in her arms with ownership, seeking to intimidate Verity further.

He saw an ugly glimmer of determination in Julie's eyes as she lifted her head and looked directly at Verity. "The kid's just tired. It's probably past her bedtime. Isn't that right, sweet girl?"

Naomi pushed away from Julie, stretching toward Leviticus, sobbing her heart out. But Julie wasn't finished with them yet. He could see it in the set of her mouth, the way her eyes watched Leviticus and Verity's reactions to her being there.

Julie hiked Naomi up higher on her hip and turned toward Leviticus. "Now, before we end this family reunion, let me ask. Does your little Amish wifey know about you joining the army and going to Afghanistan?"

Verity gasped, her hand flying to her mouth.

Julie smiled. "I didn't think so. Shame you weren't honest with her. You think she's going to be okay with you killing all those men and that young kid while you were over there?"

Pale and shaking uncontrollably, Verity looked as if she was going into shock. Leviticus walked over to her and tried to guide her to a chair, but Verity jerked her arm away, her gaze condemning, her stance rigid.

A manila folder of papers slid across the table and hit Leviticus on the arm. A pen marked with a law office's logo lay on top.

Julie spoke up, satisfaction etched on her face. "They're legal documents. Sign them and I won't call the police and report you for kidnapping."

"I'm not signing anything." Leviticus advanced toward Julie, reaching for Naomi.

"Look, Huckleberry. You can either sign or go to jail." The lawyer jumped up and sidestepped in front of Leviticus. "It's your choice." He smiled at Julie. "Miss Hernandez has every right to see her daughter, spend time with her as often as she likes. You took the child known as Naomi out of the state illegally, without her mother's consent. Unless you have a court decree granting you full custody from the state of Washington, DC, and a psychiatrist saying you're of sound mind, I strongly suggest you sign the papers and let us be on our way."

The urge to break the nose on Maxwell Horthorn's long, wrinkled face rose to a screaming crescendo in his head. He struggled to forget the ways he'd been taught to kill a man with one blow. He sought Julie's gaze. "Leave Naomi with me as we agreed and get out of this house. Make sure you take your pretty boy with you."

"Oh, honey. I plan on leaving, but not alone. Naomi goes with me. Women are prone to changing their minds. You ought to know that by now." Julie smiled sweetly at Naomi. "I want Naomi. We belong together, don't we, sugar?"

Leviticus rubbed his hands down his pant legs. *Be calm. Breathe.* He could see it in her eyes. Julie wanted him to put hands on Horthorn, kick them both out with brute strength and fury. She'd love having him arrested for violence. It was part of her plan. But he wouldn't play along. He didn't play those games anymore.

He walked toward her, hoping his angry expression might intimidate her. "I've enjoyed seeing you about as much as having a root canal. Now, give me Naomi and get out."

Clutching the whimpering child closer, Julie turned to her lawyer. "Come on. Let's go. I have what I came for."

Leviticus stood firm, not moving. "I mean it, Julie. You're not taking my daughter."

"Watch me." Her brow rose, perfectly arched. Furrows of rage marred her perfectly made-up face. "I know you better than you think. You're not man enough to deal with the threat of prison hanging over your head. You stop me and there'll be no chance of you ever seeing the kid again."

"The child's name is Naomi."

Julie handed her bulky purse to Horthorn and took a step forward and then another, testing the waters. "That old-fashioned name's not going to last long. I let you call her Naomi at first, but I'm having her name changed on Monday. I think Izzy's a pretty name. Don't you?"

"You can't do that!" Verity cried out.

Naomi recaptured Verity's gaze. Tears darkened the Amish woman's thick lashes.

Julie moved toward Leviticus, her assured smile piercing him to the bone. "I can and will take her. Without your name on the birth certificate, you don't have a leg to stand on and you know it."

Reality punched him hard in the chest, robbing him of air. "But you said you didn't want her, that your job—" He hated the way his voice trembled, exposing his doubt, giving her the edge she wanted.

Julie's eyes narrowed to slits. "You know me better than that, sugar. I said a lot of things I didn't mean while we were together." Laughing, she thrust out her left hand, showing off an engagement ring clustered with sparkling diamonds and rubies. “My fiancé really wants kids. He’ll like this one.”

She glanced around at the simple dinner table, at the old cookstove. “Look at this place. Can you really say you want our little girl raised in this hovel, around Amish people who don’t have a clue what the real world’s all about? I’ll get custody one way or the other. It doesn’t matter how. I’m happy to fight dirty. It’s the way I like to win.” She hitched Naomi higher on her slim hip. “Now get out of my way. We want to be on the road before the traffic gets heavy.”

“I could just take her from you, you know.” He continued to hold his ground, rigid and unwavering.

“I’m sure the pictures of you tearing a crying child from her mother’s arms would be very revealing to the judge. You got your phone handy, Max?”

“Right here.”

Leviticus’s legs tried to give way under

him. "This isn't the end. We'll have our day in court and you'll lose."

Her dark eyes sparkled with victory. "We'll see." She brushed past him, her heels clicking, her head held high.

He swallowed a lump the size of a fist restricting his throat. "You can count on me being there."

Naomi reached out her arms to Verity. "*Mamm!*" But then she and Julie disappeared through the back door and into the shadows of dusk.

Calm and collected, Maxwell Horthorn sauntered past and through the door. He paused, one foot still in the kitchen. "Don't fight Julie on this. Her mind is made up and you know what she's like when her back's up. She always wins. She'd love to have you arrested for kidnapping."

The screen door slammed shut in Leviticus's face.

Bewildered, his anxiety building, Leviticus stumbled over to the kitchen window and watched as Julie deftly snapped his howling child into an expensive-looking car seat wedged into the back of the car and slipped in beside her. Determination strengthened his resolve. He'd get Naomi back. He didn't know how, but he'd find a way with *Gott*'s help.

He turned to Verity, but she was already out of the room, moving fast down the hall.

He reached out for her, tried to grab her arm, but she evaded him, her back against the door of his father's bedroom. "Don't you touch me. Nothing you can say will explain away what I've just heard. Our little girl is gone because of you. You should have protected her, made sure she was safe from the likes of her."

Leviticus let his hand drop, watched as Verity turned and ran, using the walls to hold her up until she slipped into her room. As soon as the door slammed shut, he heard her wail, heard her banging her fist against the door. "My *boppli*!"

Leviticus shook all over, his heart ripped from his chest.

"*Gott*, help me. What have I done?"

Chapter Eighteen

Only a few people were on the beach. Most who weren't clearing away rubble from the storm stood in line at small food trucks, waiting on burgers to fry or ice cream to be topped with chunks of chocolate or sugar-covered licorice. Desperate to be away from the grove for a few hours, Verity found a clean spot and settled herself and Faith on a homemade quilt.

"When's my new *daed* coming home?" The sun straight overhead beat down on them. Faith let sand run through her fingers as she squinted up, waiting for her mother's reply.

Verity smiled down at her, adjusted the

kapp on her daughter's head. How should she answer the child? She stared out and watched an ocean wave as it raced onshore, piled high with froth, only to stop inches from her bare feet. "Soon, I'm sure." But she wasn't sure. The only thing she was sure of was that she missed Naomi with all her heart and couldn't understand how Leviticus could let something so horrific happen to their little girl.

She'd been forced to lie about where Naomi was at bedtime and again this morning. It broke her heart, but the lie was better than trying to explain the truth. There was no explanation that made sense.

"He and Naomi have been gone a long time. Days and days."

Verity fought tears threatening to flow. "Not so long, bumpkin. Just overnight." Verity held back her true feelings. She was glad Leviticus had still been gone when she got up, hoped he'd left Pinecraft. Leviticus had kept so many secrets. Done so many horrible things, and now the child paid the price.

She sighed, drew salty air into her lungs. As far as Faith knew, Naomi was still visiting *familye* so the two of them could have a special day on the beach. It had been the best she could come up with in the moment. Her mind still whirled with the harsh realities of life. Naomi could be gone forever. What would she tell Faith as time slipped past and Naomi never came back?

And Leviticus's past. What was she to think? What did *Gott* think of his past actions? Killing was a sin. He'd killed a child, if Julie was telling the truth. All this misery was Leviticus's fault. If only he'd confessed, told her what had been troubling him. But she was tired of thinking about his lack of forethought concerning Naomi, about the war he'd fought in. She wouldn't wonder about the circumstances surrounding the killings that had taken place during the war. She had tormented herself enough last night with what-ifs and if-onlys.

A brisk wind blew, kicking up sand in Faith's face. Verity smiled as her *dochder* fanned it away, her young *kind*'s frown expressing irritation at being distracted from the sandcastle she was building with a shovel and bucket. But then Faith smiled and scrambled up. "Theda! I didn't know you were coming to our day at the beach."

Theda Fischer strolled up arm in arm with Otto, who looked like an *Englischer* in his rolled-up pant legs and bare feet, the straw hat on his head and his beard the only giveaway that he was truly Amish.

"*Guder mariye*, Verity. You're looking very rosy-cheeked under the warm morning sun." Theda accepted Otto's arm as he helped his wife settle next to Verity.

Otto offered Faith his hand and helped her to her feet. "Let's you and I go chase seagulls while the ladies talk about all things Thanksgiving. That subject is much too boring for us, ain't so?"

Faith nodded and then waved goodbye and scurried along beside Otto, her small bare feet kicking up sand.

"I would have thought you'd be home preparing pie for tomorrow." Theda reverted to her native tongue of Pennsylvania Dutch, the language she'd first learned at her mother's knee.

Verity used her hand to shield her eyes from the sun. Dressed in a plain blue dress with an apron of starched white cotton, the older woman looked her over with compassionate eyes. This was no chance meeting. Clara must have gotten word to Theda about Naomi being whisked away by her birth mother. She needed help understanding why *Gott* would let such a thing happen.

"The pies are ready. I cooked most of them through the night."

"No sleep for the weary?"

"Nee." Verity brushed sand from the edge of her dress, doing her best to avoid Theda's scrutiny.

The older woman grasped Verity's hand and held on tight. "I'm told all is not well on the grove."

Humiliation flushed her cheeks hot. She'd been such a fool.

Theda patted Verity's hand. A sweet smile curved her lips. "You're not mad at Leviticus, are you? You should be angry at the situation you and Leviticus find yourselves in. Ain't so?"

Verity watched Faith running ahead of Otto as they headed for the ice-cream shack. No doubt the *kind* had convinced Otto an ice-cream cone would make the day special.

"I'm angry at Leviticus and the woman who birthed Naomi, but mostly at myself for being such a *bensel* and believing his lies."

"True enough he didn't talk to you about his past, but he didn't cause Naomi's mother to come and get her."

"No, but lies of omission are still lies. There were things I should have known, things that would have made a difference to Otto's decision making about marriage. He would have never asked me to get into an arranged marriage with Leviticus if he had known about the things that man has done in the past."

"Otto did know."

Verity pulled her hand away, putting space between them.

From a distance, Verity heard Faith's burst of laughter. She looked down the shoreline, searching among the few children playing in the surf. His legs as short as a boy's, Otto ran after a scurrying seagull and managed to miss its tail feathers by inches. "Otto knew and didn't tell me my future husband was a murderer?"

Gray clouds gathered overhead. The wind picked up. Red riotous curls peppered with gray danced under the *kapp* Theda had tied with her ribbons to keep it on. Her sagging jowls reminded Verity how old Theda was as she kept her gaze on her.

"Yes, he knew. Before Albert had his last stroke, Leviticus came to see us late one night. He was perplexed about the future, concerned he'd done more harm than good by returning home. Otto gave him sound advice. Prayed with him and sent him home."

Verity sat up very straight, her mind racing. How could it be? Leviticus had confessed his sins to Otto, and still her bishop arranged a marriage of convenience between them? "He knew about everything?"

"*Nee*, not everything. But the most important aspects of Leviticus's life with the *Englisch*. I heard a portion of the conversation, but not enough to form an opinion of my own. As I usually do, I trusted Otto to know what was best."

"Faith and I deserved better than a man who carried a gun and used it when he deemed necessary. Lives were lost. He played at being *Gott*."

"*Ya*, lives might have been lost. Leviticus could have died from his wounds, too."

Verity sucked in her breath, her heart pounding against her ribs. "Another fact he kept from me. I didn't know he'd been injured."

"Would you have rather he stayed in the *Englisch* world, died from his wounds without *Gott*'s forgiveness?"

"Of course not. I wish for no man to meet *Gott* with sin in his heart."

"*Gott* in His mercy saved Leviticus for another purpose. Perhaps the purpose of bringing joy and love back into your life. It is time for Leviticus to come back to the *Leit*, be forgiven for sins committed while a foolhardy *bu*."

"He's not a *bu* any longer. He's a man. A very foolish man."

Theda shook her head, disappointment creasing her forehead. "And you are too *gut* to forgive him, even though *Gott* saw fit to forgive it all?"

Verity did nothing to hold back the tears. Shame made her face flame. "I've prayed for *Gott* to help me forgive and forget, spent hours last night trying to understand, make concessions for Leviticus, but nothing makes sense to me. How could he take lives in a war that wasn't his, put his *dochder* at risk? There were no legal papers drawn up. Only a verbal agreement with Julie. He's smarter than that. And now that woman has every right to take Naomi, and there is nothing we can do to keep her with us."

"You have never made impulsive moves, never sinned, never told a lie? I'm certain-sure I have, no matter how hard I try to stay true to the *Ordnung* and stand blameless before *Gott*. A *fraa*'s job is to be always by her husband's side. You didn't stand by Leviticus when he needed you the most. Perhaps you know better than *Gott*, Verity? Perhaps your *mamm* failed to teach you that forgiveness is blessed? Are you too proud to be married to a man who has sinned in the past and asked forgiveness of his community, his *Gott*? Perhaps you see yourself as too important for a man such as this. Do you hold Leviticus to a higher standard because he disappointed you all those years ago?"

Faith came running up to her mother and thrust out her hand. "Look. We found a sand dollar. It's a little broken, but Otto said *Gott* loves broken things."

That small voice deep inside her head spoke so clearly as she held the less-than-perfect sand dollar. *Leviticus is like this sea creature. He's broken but precious to* Gott.

Otto gave Theda a hand up.

"Think on the things we spoke about," she said, brushing down her skirt and apron.

Verity nodded, too ashamed to look up. She wiped a tear from her eye and then two.

"Are you crying, *Mamm*?" Faith hugged her mother around the shoulders.

"*Nee*, my precious. I'm not crying. There's sand in my eyes. Now let's go home and get ready for Albert's return. There's a meal to cook and I'm going to need your help with the salad."

The plush chair was the most comfortable he'd ever sat in, but still Leviticus squirmed. A lot rode on this visit to Otto's lawyer. Verity sat across from him, her legs crossed at the ankles, head down, as she stared unseeing at a magazine cover turned wrong side up. They'd spoken briefly when he'd returned home the night before but said nothing about the previous night or how she felt about the things she'd learned that he'd done or hadn't done. He had no idea where things stood between them, but if he took a guess, he'd probably be more heartsick than he was already.

Otto roamed the large office, glancing at pictures of horses in meadows, of wildflowers and ladies in sun bonnets on rugs in green meadows.

Seated behind a large wooden desk littered with cream-colored files and legal books, the middle-aged secretary, who'd been ignoring them for the last hour, fanned herself with a folder and then suddenly jumped from her swivel chair like a bee had just stung her on her backside. "Mr. Glass can see you now."

She curtly acknowledged Otto with a nod as he approached, then promptly turned her back on him, her concentration now on the silver laptop screen in front of her.

Verity sprang up and led the way across the carpeted room. Leviticus hesitated, his throat restricting his breathing. His stomach clenched as he took Verity's elbow and accompanied her toward the office door, doing his best to reach Otto before they went in. *Am I doing the right thing?* Leaning in close to Otto's ear, he whispered, "You certain-sure I can trust Sam Glass with the whole truth?"

Otto guffawed. "*Ya*, sure you can. He's been a real help to the community over the years." The tips of his fingers scratched his gray-speckled beard while opening the lawyer's office door.

Otto with a nervous tic? Not a good sign.

Otto cleared his throat, glanced past Leviticus to Verity, who flashed a brave smile. "Believe it or not, even we Amish have the need of a lawyer on occasion."

Otto turned the knob on the door and it swung open wide. A tall balding man rose from a plush leather chair. "Well, look who the wind's blown in." He smiled, exposing straight white teeth that were obviously fake. His hand extended, he greeted Otto with a friendly smile and warm handshake.

Otto returned the man's smile. "*Danki*

for seeing us on such short notice, Sam. It's been too long."

"Too long indeed." The two older men slapped each other on the back affectionately, giving Leviticus the impression that they had been friends for a long time. They chatted robustly about family matters and then shifted their friendly banter to the lousy weather they'd been having, and the cost of the city cleanup.

Leviticus thought of the dwindling amount in his bank account. The grove was fast becoming a money pit and he didn't have a clue what this meeting was going to cost him, but it had been two days since Julie had shown up and snatched away his daughter. He'd get Naomi back no matter the cost or what he had to do. He rolled his shoulders, trying to ease some of the tension building in his upper back and neck.

Otto pointed Leviticus's way. "This here is Leviticus Hilty, one of Pinecraft's faithful."

Leviticus took the lawyer's extended hand.

"You must be Albert's son."

"I am." He accepted Sam's friendly pat on the back.

"Your father and I go way back. I heard he'd been ill. Is he doing better?"

Relief about Albert coming home had Leviticus grinning from ear to ear. "He is. Mose is bringing him home this afternoon while we're out."

Sam Glass smiled. "Just in time for Thanksgiving. Good, good. And this pretty lady must be your wife."

"Ya." It was the first time he'd had the opportunity to claim Verity as his own. Pride made his chest swell as he watched her delicate hand be engulfed by Sam's tanned paw.

Sam's smile was polite as he pointed toward three empty chairs near the big desk in the center of the room. "Let's all get comfortable. Anyone want a cup of coffee or bottle of water before we get started?" Sam's alert brown eyes focused on Verity and then Leviticus.

Otto answered for them. "*Nee*, nothing for

us. But you go ahead. I know how much you like your coffee."

Grabbing a disposable cup of hot brew from the coffee maker behind him, Sam once again made himself comfortable in his chair and refocused his attention back on them. "So, what's up? Sale of a house go wrong?"

Leviticus leaned forward, sitting on the edge of the plush leather chair he'd settled in. "It's my daughter…our daughter Naomi. Her birth mother, Julie Hernandez, came and took her and we want her back."

"You two have primary custody of the child?" Sam scribbled on the pad in front of him.

Leviticus dropped his chin. He hated that Verity had to hear all the stupid things he had done before coming home. "No, but I had a verbal agreement with Julie. When she found out she was pregnant, she agreed not to give the child up for adoption if I promised to raise it without her.

"When I returned from my tour in Afghanistan, Naomi had been born and was being cared for by a full-time nanny. Julie came home two days later and seemed glad to relinquish custody of Naomi to me without complaint or hesitation. I came down to Pinecraft with my *dochder*, so she could be raised Amish and get to know my family."

"Before that, had this woman always kept her word to you?"

"More or less. I had no reason to think she wasn't serious about not wanting the *kind*... until yesterday when she showed up at our door with an attorney."

"I assume you made sure your name was on the child's birth certificate?"

Leviticus glanced at Verity. Her head was down, her hands neatly folded in her lap. Where did she get her strength? "I thought it was. When I asked to see the document, she made up some excuse about Naomi's name being spelled wrong and how she'd send me a copy. Yesterday was the first time I saw the amended copy. My name was nowhere on it, and the lawyer said I could easily be charged with kidnapping." He cleared his throat, repositioned himself in his seat. He took a nervous glance Verity's way. She sat looking straight ahead, as if she'd rather be anywhere than this office hearing what a fool he had been.

"There was no short-term marriage between you and this woman?"

Leviticus answered. *"Nee."*

Sam's informal demeanor evaporated. He was all business now. "I thought Amish folk married before they started a family."

Otto cleared his throat, his fingers tugging at his beard. Verity slumped in her chair as if in pain. "We usually do, but Leviticus wasn't a member of the church at the time the *kind* was conceived."

"Ah."

Leviticus loathed what he was about to admit, especially with Verity listening. "Julie and I were sharing an apartment, living together, but only for a short time."

"You live with her for more than six months? Ever refer to her as your wife?"

"*Nee.* Our relationship wasn't like that."

"What was it like?"

If the floor had opened and swallowed him, Leviticus would have been happy to fall in the hole.

Otto sat grim-faced, listening to Leviticus's words, disapproval washing out his complexion. He'd been told the bare facts weeks ago, but now the whole story of Naomi's conception was coming out. He tapped his fingers against the leather arm of his chair.

"I was in the army at the time and living the life, if you know what I mean."

Sam's head bobbed. "I do. These things happen. But you were honorably discharged?"

"*Ya.*"

"Good. That's a plus. You supported your child?"

"I did while I was away, and during the time I was in the hospital recuperating from my wounds." Leviticus saw Verity's head turn away from him. "Once I picked Naomi up, I stopped paying the nanny's wages.

There was no agreement put down on paper about child support from Julie. I thought she got on with her life. Forgot about me and the *kind* until yesterday."

"Okay." Sam scribbled several lines of information down before he spoke again. "Let me consider Florida laws and see what's going to make or break this case." He rose and gave Leviticus another bone-crunching handshake and then turned and patted Verity affectionately on the back. "Wish I had better news for you," he told Leviticus. "But you're going to have to prove paternity with a DNA test and then we'll have to fight this in courts. Parental rights cases can be messy and take a long time." Brows raised, his sympathetic gaze redirected solely on Leviticus. "As I see it, you don't have a leg to stand on, but if we can get something on this Hernandez woman, we might stand a chance."

"It's best we leave that. Julie's Naomi's birth mother. I won't slander her in public."

Sam cleared his throat. "She's happy to smear you. Why not go in for the kill? She's taken your child, lied, implied she'd have you arrested for kidnapping. But maybe you still have feelings for this woman?"

"*Nee*, nothing like that. It's just not our way." For the first time in a long time, Leviticus meant it when he said *our way*. He was a Plain man now. A man of faith. He'd put his trust in *Gott*. Plain men didn't slander women, even if they had ripped their heart out by stealing their *kinner*.

Sam walked them out, bear-hugged Otto, shook Leviticus's hand again and nodded at Verity.

Leviticus put his straw hat back on his head as he headed for the door, Verity by his side, his legs weak and trembling. "You'll let me know when you find something out?"

"Sure will."

Otto, Verity and Leviticus were silent as they strolled to the elevator. Verity hurried ahead, as if what she had heard was more than she could handle. Leviticus's heart broke for her, but then his mind went into overdrive. There was so much they needed to talk about. Why had he waited so long to confide in her? He rubbed the back of his neck. And there was Julie to contend with. She wasn't cut out to be a *mamm*. He had to find a way to get Naomi back.

Otto slowed his step. "You okay?"

Leviticus rubbed the stubble growing on his chin. *Am I okay?*

"*Nee.* I keep seeing Naomi reaching out to Verity, crying *mamm*." He threaded a hand through his hair and replaced his straw hat. He glanced up at Verity waiting for the elevator to arrive. "She loves that child as much as I do. Losing her has ripped the heart out of her. Faith doesn't understand where her little *schweschder* went and keeps asking for her." His shoulders slumped. "Julie's selfish, dedicated to her job. I can't understand her marrying a man who wants *kinner*. I had to beg her to keep the *boppli* when she found out she was pregnant. She wanted no part of being a *mamm* back then."

"Maybe she woke up to what she'd done. There has to be some good in her."

Moments later, Leviticus stepped off the elevator with Verity following close behind. He massaged the constant ache in the back of his neck. "I keep praying for *Gott*'s will, asking Him to show me what to do, but all I hear back is deafening silence."

"*Gott* has a plan for Naomi's life." Otto tugged at his beard.

"I'm trying to find peace, but I'm new at this thing called faith." And he *was* trying to be strong, for Verity's sake as much as his own.

Seconds later, they stepped into bright sunlight and meandered down the sidewalk. Leviticus, afraid to ask the bishop, spoke anyway. "What if it's not *Gott*'s will for me to have Naomi back?"

His heart pounded in his ears. Was it possible? Could the *Gott* he now served ask such a thing of him, of Verity? He chewed at his nail. Could he live without his daughter and still serve a *Gott* who allowed such a thing to happen?

"The *Ordnung* requires we trust *Gott*. It also reminds us we are His beloved children."

Leviticus's hands tightened into fists at his sides; he wished he could reach out and take Verity's hand. This situation was his fault, but she suffered for his mistakes. He couldn't fault her in any way. Naomi had become her daughter as much as his own. But somehow, they'd have to learn to accept *Gott*'s will. Were his blunders too much for her to forgive? Was he asking too much?

"You sure you two are okay?"

"*Ya*, we're okay," Leviticus said, hopeful Albert's being home would distract Verity from her worry for Naomi.

Please, Gott. *Help us find a way to accept Your will for our lives, our child's life. Don't let my growing faith veer to the right or to the left. And,* Gott, *help Verity to forgive me and find a way to love me as much as I've grown to love her.*

Chapter Nineteen

Four long tables had been pushed close together to accommodate the crowd of family and friends who'd come to celebrate Albert's blessed homecoming and Thanksgiving Day meal.

Verity seated herself in between Clara and Leviticus with a sigh. There had been a lot of last-minute things to do. Lack of sleep and more work than she could handle had her tired and not just a little grumpy.

"Verity." Leviticus nudged her. "Would you pass along the sweet potato casserole?"

"I'm sorry. Did you say something?" Verity redirected her attention her husband's way. Leviticus's arm was extended, patiently waiting, the sticky casserole dish held out for her to take. She did as she was asked, smiling her apology to Clara.

I haven't said a single word to Leviticus the whole meal. She really hadn't talked at length to anyone. She glanced down at the head of the table. Albert was seated in his place of honor, looking fit as a man could look after days of hospital care.

Verity couldn't help but notice how lackluster her husband's expression was. Like her, his thoughts were no doubt on Naomi. He was putting on a show of normalcy for his *daed*. Verity lowered her head, pushed round a slice of turkey, her appetite poor. Since learning the truth about Leviticus's past she'd spent so much time searching for understanding, for a way to forgive his secret life as a soldier and the painful loss of Naomi. Some way she had to be able to trust him again. But being Amish had taught her to forgive, helped her finally find a measure of peace. It was *Gott*'s job to deal with Leviticus's past and to bring Naomi home. Not hers. She had to lean on her faith, believe for the child's return.

Gott*'s will be done.*

From time to time, as the meal progressed, Verity heard Albert laughing out loud at the head of the table. No doubt at something one of his old cronies had said about his inability to successfully get food to his mouth. Albert's stroke might be impeding his use of a fork and his speech, but he wasn't letting his disabilities ruin his good mood or his Thanksgiving meal.

Having her father-in-law home filled her heart with joy, but for the life of her, she couldn't stop fretting over Naomi. Where was the tiny child this Thanksgiving Day?

She glanced down at Albert again, noticed how pale he still looked, but refrained from suggesting he lie down for a while. That afternoon he'd raised a fuss when he heard the day nurse's suggestion that he stay in bed during the meal. Feisty as always, he'd made it clear he was not eating turkey and dressing without his family and friends around him. He would eat at the table or not eat at all.

Not being able to use his fork properly hadn't slowed the thin old man down one bit. What didn't hit his mouth hit the floor, but she didn't care a whit about the mess he was making. She could clean up under his chair later. He was home and happy. That was all that mattered.

Albert hooted his approval when the sweet potato dish was passed his way around the table a second time. He didn't say a word, but his lopsided smile expressed his appreciation to Verity. Clara scooped a small portion of the sticky goo onto her beloved father-in-law's plate and then went back to her chair and started chatting with Solomon.

A loud knock came at the door. At the end of his table, Joe Muller, Albert's cousin, shifted in his chair. "You want me to open it?"

His mouth full of food, Albert nodded his approval.

Joe scooted out of his chair and eased the door open. His expression became confused as he spoke to whoever was at the door. He stepped back inside and closed the door most of the way. "There's a fancy *Englischer* out there, insisting on speaking to you, Leviticus."

Verity laid down her napkin, her stomach quivering, watching as Leviticus excused himself and made his way through the maze of tables and over to the door. He slipped out quickly and shut it behind him.

A chill went down Verity's spine, the memory of the last unexpected visitor at the grove haunting her.

Forks clattered against plates, the hum of the room drowning out whatever was being said on the porch. Minutes turned into what seemed a half hour. The sound of a car motor starting up drew her attention to the window.

Joe scooted away from the door as it opened wide.

Her hand raised to her mouth, Verity

smothered a gasp as Leviticus stepped across the door's threshold, holding Naomi in his arms. His gaze sought hers, tears glistening in his eyes. A genuine smile creased dimples into his face.

Verity rose, excitement filling her to overflowing. Naomi was home!

"We've got a sleepy girl here. Verity, would you help me get her ready for her nap?"

"*Ya*, sure," she muttered, pushing back her chair and almost knocking it over as she hurried to reach Leviticus's side.

Albert waved his hand, trying to utter words.

Leviticus grinned his father's way. "We'll be right back, *Daed*. You keep eating."

Verity fell over her own feet as she scurried beside Leviticus, her hand on the small child's arm. Gott *has heard our prayers. Naomi is home!*

With the push of his shoulder, Leviticus eased the children's bedroom door shut behind them.

Verity's eyes sought his, perplexed and wide with wonder. "Our *boppli* is home for *gut*?"

Leviticus nodded, his hands trembling as he laid the child in her cot. Verity reached out and lovingly touched Naomi's dark curls, her rosy cheek. Verity's shoulder leaned into Leviticus's chest for support. "I don't understand. What's happened?"

The feel of Naomi cuddled up close to him had moved him beyond any joy he'd ever experienced. "I honestly can't say what changed. All I know for sure is Maxwell Horthorn brought our *dochder* back." Leviticus picked up the folder of papers the lawyer had given him and handed them to Verity. "He gave these papers to me and assured me they were legal. Look for yourself. He said they're signed by Julie and stamped by the local magistrate. The most important paper acknowledges me as Naomi's natural father and gives you permission to adopt Naomi as your own. Julie has relinquished all parental rights to her."

"But that woman was determined to lay claim to Naomi."

Joy rushed through him. "I know. But Horthorn said Julie changed her mind. Seems her future husband dumped her, and she had no further need of Naomi." Leviticus slid his arm around Verity's shoulders, and side by side, they stood watching their *dochder* sleep. Naomi's lips puckered, her mouth nursing on an imaginary bottle.

Leviticus laughed. "Look at her. It's like she never was gone."

He watched the darkness leave Verity's eyes, saw pure joy replace it.

"I can't believe she's ours once again." She snuggled close, her face pressed against his chest.

"I need to ask your forgiveness, even though I know I don't deserve it. I've given you every reason to distrust me, but I've changed and will continue to become the man you need in your life. *Gott* has forgiven me for my transgressions, helped me to see what is important and what's not. I need your love."

"I forgive you your past, Leviticus."

He was so grateful that her Amish faith was stronger than his, and that she'd found a way to forgive him. "As far as I'm concerned, we've been a family since we said our vows." He pulled Verity closer, wrapping his arms around her waist and sighing with relief when she didn't resist his overture of affection.

Verity's eyes sought his, her look of confusion gone as he bent to softly kiss her lips.

Leviticus lifted her chin. "Please believe me when I tell you that you mean the world to me, and not just as a *mamm* for Naomi. My feelings for you go deep, so much deeper than I knew possible." He held her gaze, allowed all the love he felt for her to shine to the surface for her to see. "You and the girls have shown me what true love is. You're precious to me. I promise to never hurt you again."

Her brow furrowed, ashamed she had to

ask. “The *Englischer* world? Does it still beckon to you?”

“*Nee*, not anymore. I am a Plain Amish man now. My desire is to serve the Lord, be a *gut* husband and *dat*.”

Verity rested her forehead against his chest, her arms circling his waist. “I’ve dreamed of this moment, been too afraid to dare hope for fear you’d slip away again.”

Leviticus could feel Verity’s body trembling. “Ten years ago, I was a fool. Forgive me for leaving. Say you’ll be my love once again.”

Verity lifted her head, her love revealed in her eyes, in the sweet smile on her face. “I’ve loved you most of my life. How could that change now?”

Leviticus smiled. He’d dreamed of this moment, as well, longed for it for so long. “I promise you will always come first, that I will be a good husband and *daed* to our girls. But most of all, I promise to love you until my last breath and beyond.”

Their kiss was warm and promising. They

had time now, time to be the *familye* they both longed for. But his father awaited. "We have so much to talk about, but first we'd best get back to *Daed*. He'll be wondering."

Verity nodded, her smile bringing a glow to her face. "Do you think anyone will notice the difference in us? I feel as if our love is shining like diamonds all around us."

Leviticus laughed. "Let them wonder. This joy is ours and ours alone."

* * * * *

If you enjoyed
Their Convenient Amish Marriage,
look for these other Love Inspired titles
by Cheryl Williford:

The Amish Widow's Secret
The Amish Midwife's Courtship
Her Secret Amish Child

Dear Readers,

I can't tell you how glad I am to be writing books again and enjoying my new way of life to the fullest. The last two years have been difficult ones. I was diagnosed with an early stage carcinoma just outside my pancreas in late 2015. Seems that's not a good spot to have cancer. The only way to remove it was with a Whipple surgery, which is called the bad, bad, bad surgery. Very dangerous and difficult to recover from.

I underwent the surgery in October of that year. I don't remember a lot about those first six months, but I can tell you it wasn't fun. Spent many months in rehab, regaining my ability to eat by mouth after several months with a stomach tube. Lost forty-five pounds. Was as weak as a kitten and stupid from pain meds. Got home safe and had to completely change my way of eating, when I could stomach the thought of food.

I started five months of chemo and God,

in all His mercy, saw me through that scary period of my life. What a privilege it was to pray for others as they were fighting the good fight. The chemo made me sick, but I didn't lose all my hair. Somehow, that seemed so important at the time. The chemo also gave me "chemo brain," which kept me from writing for ages. I just couldn't concentrate and not writing didn't make me happy. I longed to be back in Pinecraft, finishing Verity and Leviticus's story.

As you can see by the book in your hand, I did finish their story, and am so thrilled to say I'm in the middle of book three of the Pinecraft Homecomings series. I'm still dealing with brain fog at times. I can tell you there's no one more miserable than a writer who can't think clearly enough to plot and write.

To God be all the glory as He heals me! To my editors, I say a heartfelt thank you and God bless you for your prayers and patience. Not having a deadline helped take away some of the stress. For all my family who prayed for me, to the people on Facebook who kept me in constant prayer, I say, thank you! My body scans are coming back clean.

I hope you've enjoyed the romance between Leviticus and Verity. Please keep an eye open for my final book in the Pinecraft Homecomings series. It's slow going, but God in His mercy, is allowing me to continue with life and my love of writing. Thank you all for being faithful readers of my work.

Believe in His mercy, for He is faithful,

Cheryl Williford